MURDER IN PARADISE

by

Larry K. and Lorna Collins

WHISKEY CREEK PRESS
www.whiskeycreekpress.com

Published by
WHISKEY CREEK PRESS

Whiskey Creek Press
PO Box 51052
Casper, WY 82605-1052
www.whiskeycreekpress.com

ISBN 978-1-60313-600-6

Credits
Cover Artist: Melissa Summers
Editor: Sylvia Anglin
Printed in the United States of America

Other Books by Authors Available at Whiskey Creek Press:

www.whiskeycreekpress.com

Murder... They Wrote - Published August 2009

What if a retired NYPD officer is asked to investigate a mysterious death at the National Authors Conference where the attendees offer theories and suspicions? ***Murder ...They Wrote*** answers this question as Agapé Jones, retired NYPD detective, tries to determine the truth surrounding the death of a noted poet and critic.

Lorna's titles:

Snowflake Secrets - Published February 2008

Prologue, Epilogue, Allegra

Can objects contain magic? The Sullivan sisters think so. On Christmas Eve 1958, Great-aunt Maude gives each of them a snowflake ornament. Years later, they learn she might have crocheted something extra into their gifts.

Seasons of Love – Published February 2009

"Winter's Song"

To Dan Jensen, life seems hopeless. But when he gets railroaded into performing in a Christmas musical, a lovely young woman named Amy Roberts provides more than musical assistance. She brings hope and the promise of new life.

Directions of Love – Published February 2010

"Finding Love in Paradise"

Best friends Kimi, Melinda, Jacque, and Lilianna grew up in Aspen Grove, Colorado, but went in separate directions after high school. Now they're invited to their twentieth high school reunion. They want to see each other again, but will they all attend, and what stories will they have to share?

An Aspen Grove Christmas **–Published December 2010**

"Mistletoe Magic"

Christmas is a magic time of year, especially when love is in the air and Aspen Grove, Colorado celebrates five weddings and a family reunion. All Noelle McGregor wants is real mistletoe her first Christmas without family, but getting it leads to literally falling for Matt Spicer.

Dedication

This book is dedicated to:

- Coleman "Love" Smith, the inspiration for Agapé
- Angela, who keeps him in line
- And the Kihei Canoe Club

Aloha,
from beautiful
Oahu, a little bit
of Paradise!
Mahalo and God
bless!
Jay K. Collins
Laura Collins

Acknowledgements:

With *mahalo* and much *aloha*, we would like to thank:

- **Lagunita Writers Group** – As always, you kept us going, provided suggestions, and made us think about new ways to look at the story. We're very grateful to all of you, especially our hostess with the cookies, Martha Anderson.
- **Our Family and Friends** – Your support and encouragement have meant so much. If we could pick, we'd still pick you.
- **Darcy Bowen** – To the best secret proofreader, our profound gratitude. You catch the things we don't, and you enjoy our work. What more could we ask?
- **Love & Angela Smith, Lovie Cooper, Nicki Weaver, and Robert Schwenck** (the real artist) – You have inspired and informed our characters, and we hope our sincere affection for all of you shows in the writing.
- **The Kihei Canoe Club** – Thanks for showing us around, taking Larry out for a paddle, and generally encouraging our writing. We still can't believe that Love was already doing what we'd 'invented' for our character!
- **Whiskey Creek Press**, especially **Debi** and **Steve Womack**, **Melissa Summers**, our wonderful Editors Sylvia Anglin and Marsha Briscoe, and **Linda Voth** of **PawPrints** - Your support and friendship have been immense blessings.
- **EPIC** – We are blessed to be part of this special group of

e-publishing professionals. Thanks for letting us lead the workshops and take part in all the activities. And thanks for being friends, too.

- **Kay & Raul Lopez** – If you hadn't moved to Hawaii and Raul hadn't taken up outrigger paddling, Agapé wouldn't have either. Thanks for the background information and for all the years of very special friendship.
- **Steve Boehne** of **Infinity Surfboards** – Thank you for all the technical information on surfboard construction, letting Larry invade your shaping room to take part in the process, and building him the greatest boards he's ever ridden.
- Lorna thanks **Larry** – For 'birthing' this one with me. It was so much fun figuring out how to resolve plot issues together. Can't wait to start on the next one! Writing with you is one of the most enjoyable things we've done. I love you more than ever.
- Larry would like to thank **Lorna** – For another fun trip through Hawaiian waters again with Agapé and company. For adding the heart into our characters and correcting my horrendous spelling and punctuation. All my love.

Chapter 1: Morning Paddle Interrupted

Guess I'm getting used to this early morning routine, I thought as I stood on the dock at the entrance to Lahaina Harbor with the other members of my team, paddle in hand. My friend, Kimo Akai, had persuaded me, Agapé Jones, retired NYPD detective, that it would be fun to try outrigger canoe racing. Right now I had my doubts.

Kimo and his cousin, Keoki, guided the six-man craft to the dock and I eased my bum leg into position at third spot in the boat. The bullet I'd taken in the thigh, which ended my career with the NYPD, would never let me run again, but my arms were still strong even for my sixty-plus years. Of course, Kimo is at least two decades younger and Keoki nearly three.

"You won't be the oldest on the team," Kimo had assured me. "That honor falls to Raul. He's a full eighteen months ahead of you. We jokingly call him the 'old man,' but he can still out-paddle any of us."

The trade winds were down, leaving the ocean glassy

smooth as we headed out the harbor entrance. I counted my strokes: *twelve, thirteen.* The steerer shouted "*Ae*!" and we responded with "*Ho*!" and shifted our paddles to the opposite side. The craft moved easily through the calm waters. It would be much harder later in the day when the trades made the surface choppy.

Several surfers were enjoying the reefs north of the entrance. I envied their ability to leap quickly to their feet and duck into the steepening waves. With skill and some luck, the surfer would exit 'the tube,' as they called it, into the calm deeper waters of the entrance channel just as the liquid wall collapsed. A rider too far back or not quick enough would have to contend with the shallow, board-hungry reef.

Keoki steered the canoe south. It would take a couple of hours to make the harbor at Maalaea our goal.

Twelve, thirteen, "Ho!" shift.

The hills behind Lahaina shone brightly in the morning light. Several columns of ruddy brown smoke boiled skyward in the still air. Cane fields were being burned in preparation for harvest. Burning cleared the leaves and insects, leaving the sweet, juice-filled stalks ready for cutting.

Better concentrate on paddling, Agapé, I reminded myself after missing a switch and clicking oars with Raul.

The 'old man' in the number two spot raised an eyebrow but didn't say anything.

About half an hour into the trip and a mile from shore, Keoki called out, "Hey, what's dat ova dere?" and turned the outrigger toward a floating object ahead. As we approached, I recognized it as a body, face down, still attached by an ankle-leash to a short surfboard. I heard groans and gasps as the others realized what we'd found.

Keoki guided us to bring the body between the canoe and its outrigger. Kimo crawled out on the forward spar and gingerly turned the victim over. It was a young man. A couple of the guys said, "Oh, no," and one said, "It can't be."

During my years with NYPD, I had seen bodies in the harbor, Central Park, and the East River. I'd have guessed this one to have been in the water a few hours rather than days because there was no significant bloating. There appeared to be a puncture wound in his chest.

"Kimo," I directed, "drag the body over here. We can load him in the center of the canoe."

He gave me a horrified look.

"We have to do something. We can't just leave him here."

My friend still appeared reluctant but used the surfboard to nudge the victim toward me. Aside from a death at a conference last year, Kimo, as hotel activities director, probably hadn't had much contact with corpses. I'd had far too much.

Raul looked ashen but helped me lift the victim onboard. Keoki attached the leash to the rear spar. The surfboard would trail along behind the canoe.

I pulled a zippered plastic bag from my pocket and extracted my cell phone, grateful my wife, Gerry, had insisted I bring it this morning. "Damn, no signal. We'll have to get closer to the beach."

We headed for shore with our additional 'passenger.' No one spoke.

As soon as the bars appeared on my cell, I hit the speed dial to Kimo's uncle, Detective George "Duke" Wimakinu-kalulani. I had worked on a previous case with the man and still had his number. He answered immediately.

"Agapé Jones here," I announced. "We've found a body floating about a mile off Olowalu. Can you have your people meet us at Launiupoko Beach? We're in an outrigger canoe and headed in right now."

"I'm on it," he said. "I'll have forensics and the coroner meet you there. See you in a few minutes."

Police vehicles lined the highway and parking area as we made our way through the surf and pulled the outrigger up on dry sand. We were immediately surrounded by uniformed officers while others kept curious onlookers away. I motioned our crew back and let the authorities take over.

The chief investigator's car pulled up and the "big man" himself got out. The term usually refers to the person's position or office. But for Chief Detective Duke, at six-foot-four with a linebacker build, it was literal. He easily dwarfed the others standing nearby.

"Well, Agapé, seems like we've done this before," Duke remarked as he approached, disposable coffee cup in hand. The big guy was referring to the first time we'd met at the National Authors Conference, standing over another corpse. He looked down at the body and sucked air through gritted teeth. A serious look crossed his face.

"When you called, I was afraid this is who it was."

"Who do you mean?" I asked.

"Don't you watch television? It's been on all the news programs. Professional surfer Philip Fowler, son of State Senator Thomas Fowler, went missing on Oahu three days ago."

"I don't watch much TV," I confessed. "I've gained a few pounds. Gerry thought I was turning into a couch potato and restricted my viewing to a few favorite sports programs and cop shows."

"Well, the senator's been on all the channels. Even offered a ten thousand dollar reward for his son's safe return. This will be tough on him."

"Hi, Pops," Keoki said as he approached.

"Keoki, you part of this group?" Duke asked.

"Sure. Kimo talked me into joining. Said it would help my stamina for surfing."

I noticed the son's usual pidgin slang had all but disappeared when speaking to his dad.

"You think that's Flip?" he continued. "I was afraid it might be, same hair and build. I met him once, at a contest on Oahu. Seemed like a nice guy, for a *haole*."

"We'll know as soon as forensics can verify it. Till then, you're not to talk to anyone about this. Hear me?"

"Loud and clear, Pops," Keoki responded.

Statements were taken from the team and we were admonished to not discuss our discovery with anyone, especially not the media, until an official police press statement was released. I wished I'd had my trusty notebook, but it was home on the dresser. Instead, I tried to memorize the observations I'd made to write down later.

No one felt like continuing the run, so Kimo called the canoe club on my cell and arranged for us and the outrigger to be picked up.

On the drive back, questions formed in my mind. *How would a surfer who disappeared on Oahu three days ago end up floating off Maui? Too far to drift, even if the current was in this direction. The area off Olowalu is noted for tiger sharks. Why didn't they attack? Was it an accident or was he killed? If so, did the killer think the sharks would destroy the evidence? If he wasn't bleeding, maybe the sharks didn't smell him. If I knew how he got here, I might be able to figure out how he died.*

Chapter 2: Special Investigator

By the time I returned home to Kihei, I was exhausted. I'd forgotten the emotional strain caused by the death of a young person. Somehow, when older folks die, even under questionable circumstances, the tragedy doesn't seem quite as great. They've at least had a chance to make choices and spend some years in this world. But seeing a young man killed before his life has really begun is heartbreaking.

I slumped into my chair in front of the TV. It wasn't my old leather recliner, but Gerry had insisted that in this house all the furniture had to match. That meant wicker. I missed the old one. Even though the rocking chair was comfortable enough, it wasn't as cozy as my well-worn leather favorite.

Absently, I began channel surfing. It was still before noon and there wasn't much on.

The second time around, the news caught my eye. I thought they might have some coverage of our discovery.

The lead story was about the upcoming outrigger races. Fiji had beaten the Hawaiian teams the last two years. I knew we were all determined to win back the championship in this round.

This was followed by stories on other local sports, which I ignored. After the commercial came a report on the continuing North Shore controversy.

"Developers attempted to obtain permits for the construction of a proposed hotel and retail complex to be built near the current resort at Turtle Bay. Protesters shouted threats and attempted to stop representatives of the builders from entering the hearing at the Department of Public Works. Following a scuffle, authorities arrested several demonstrators. This is Simon Ochoa reporting from Hale'iwa."

The announcer came back on camera. "On another front, police announced today that more shark carcasses without fins washed up on Mokul'ia Beach. Although shark finning has been illegal in Hawaii since 2000, authorities fear that high Asian demand and escalating prices may have triggered a resurgence of the practice. Police are..."

Suddenly, a news bulletin crossed the screen and I sat forward.

A family photo appeared, the kind posed with the beach in the background, often sent as Christmas cards.

I recognized the handsome, blond young man as the same one whose body we had recovered earlier. He sat on a large rock in front of a beautiful woman whose skin was the color of warm hot chocolate with lots of cream. She had round black eyes, long sleek black hair and a full mouth—the look I think of as Hawaiian. Both her hands rested on his shoulders.

Standing next to her, I recognized State Senator Fowler. His blond hair, graying at the temples, was unruffled. Accentuated by his even tan, his grin revealed perfect white teeth. He was dressed in a neatly-pressed Hawaiian shirt in shades of blue and gray, conservative with a muted design. In front of him sat a good-looking young man who resembled the woman. The senator's hand gripped his arm.

The label below the photo stated, "Senator Fowler and Family."

I was immediately struck by the interpersonal dynamics. As a cop, I was trained to read body language, but even a civilian could spot something wrong here.

The only contact 'Dad' had was with the son in front of him and his upper body was turned slightly away from his wife. 'Mom' looked serious and almost protective of the blond kid, and there appeared to be little connection between the two boys.

The next picture showed Philip with tousled hair standing next to his surfboard, grinning at the camera. The announcer said it was taken when he won the Pipeline Masters contest several months earlier. "Stand by for breaking news."

Detective Duke appeared onscreen.

"Good morning." Duke's full name appeared in the crawl below.

"At approximately nine o'clock this morning, a body was discovered floating in the water off the coast of Maui. It has tentatively been identified as Philip Fowler, the missing younger son of Senator Thomas Fowler. Cause of death is expected following the results of an autopsy. We are unable to provide any additional information at this time. Thank you."

The reporters shouted questions at Duke's retreating back, but he was through.

Every local channel was covering the story, discussing what might have happened. All I wanted was escape.

I finally found a baseball game but couldn't concentrate on it. A young man was dead, and the question of how it happened wouldn't leave me alone.

"You're home early," Gerry said as she placed grocery bags on the kitchen counter. "I thought you and the guys were going to the Kihei Café after your paddle."

"Yeah, but practice was cut short." I didn't want to talk about it, and I was sure she didn't want to hear about it either. My wife was relieved when I got out of police work and wouldn't be happy if she thought I might be involved in anything dangerous, especially murder.

She said, "I was going to make myself a tuna salad with iced tea. Care to join me?"

"Sounds good."

I watched her start getting things ready, admiring her efficiency. I wouldn't starve if I had to cook for myself, but I wouldn't eat very well either. And I was glad, as always, to have her in charge.

Actually, even after more than forty years of marriage, I still love watching her move. She studied ballet as a girl and still has the ease and grace of a dancer. Her unlined latté-colored skin makes it hard for me to believe she isn't the bride I married. Of course, I'm reminded of the passing years every morning when I look in the mirror and see my wrinkled, dark brown, shoe-leather skin and salt-and-pepper nappy hair.

"Enough daydreaming," she said as she handed me some silverware. "Make yourself useful."

I set the table on the lanai while she continued working in the kitchen. I enjoy the outdoor lifestyle of Hawaii and take advantage of it whenever possible.

We'd just sat down when my cell phone rang. I was grateful for our grandson who had reprogrammed it at Christmas. I still wondered if the theme from *Jaws* was an improvement over *Beverly Hills Cop,* which had plagued me last year. But at least it was a change.

"Jones here." It was a habit from my years on the force.

"Agapé, glad you're there." I recognized Duke's voice and got up to take the call inside. "I just got off the phone with Senator Fowler. He wants a special investigator assigned to the case and I recommended you since you're the best detective in the islands. He says he'll pay a thousand a week, plus all your expenses until the case is solved."

"Gerry won't be pleased about this." At the same time my heart was beating faster and I realized how badly I needed to know what had happened. "I'll get back to you."

"I need your answer no later than two this afternoon. The Senator insisted on a meeting in Honolulu first thing tomorrow morning."

"That's not much time."

"He's an impatient man. His son is dead, and he wants answers."

"I have to think about this." It would mean being away from home for who knew how long. The only real commitment I had was practicing with the team. We were training for a contest in a few weeks and needed to improve our strength and coordination. Timing is everything. Missing a couple of practices probably wouldn't be too much of a problem, but I'd lose a lot of the strength and technique I'd gained if I didn't stay with it.

"You have until two o'clock. Then I'll have to locate somebody else. No one here has your skills, but I'll dig up someone if I have to."

"I'll let you know right away."

I was intrigued. If I were honest, I was also flattered that they wanted me. Now all I had to do was convince Gerry.

Chapter 3: The Interview

The early morning flight to Oahu was uneventful. I was thankful for the plastic cup of guava juice provided by the airline. Not only was it tasty, the natural sugar gave me a slight energy boost. I had missed my morning coffee, and the swill the airline served with the little packets of dried-cream stuff just didn't satisfy. Besides, on a twenty-minute flight, there's hardly time for the attendants to distribute the cups before having to collect trash for landing. Still, I was missing the breakfast I should have been enjoying on my lanai with Gerry.

Convincing my wife the previous day of the need to help the police, even in an advisory capacity, had been as difficult as I'd anticipated.

"But you're retired," she objected several times during the discussion. "You're not getting into any dangerous work, are you?"

"No," I insisted. "I'm just helping Detective Duke with investigative procedures, evidence gathering protocol, that kind of thing. Police in Hawaii don't get many high-profile cases, and Duke wanted me to train their people in some of the NYPD procedures." I didn't tell her I would be the special investigator.

She grudgingly acknowledged I could be of help. But I knew she was nervous. Her memories of the years at home in New York waiting for my return each day still haunted her.

There are two kinds of police officers' wives: one wants to know everything, usually keeping a radio scanner on all day; the other doesn't want to know anything. Gerry was the second.

As I descended the stairway to Baggage Claim, I spotted a large man in a dark blue shirt and pants holding a small sign with my name. I identified myself.

"You're here. Good," he said. "The car's right outside. Any bags?"

"Just one, but I can handle it." I spotted it on the carousel, picked it up, and followed him.

The car turned out to be a white Cadillac stretch limo, vintage early nineties, with burl wood and dark leather interior and privacy windows featuring a map of the islands etched on the glass. Very classy. A PIMPMOBILE!

"I've been instructed to take you directly to the house. It should take about forty minutes to get to Hawai'i Kai. Just relax. If you need anything, speak into the intercom. My name is Clarence."

"Clarence. And your last name?"

"It's Washington, sir. Clarence Washington."

"Nice to meet you, Clarence Washington. Been working

for the Fowler family long?"

"'Bout ten years, ever since the senator entered politics," he answered as we pulled away from the curb.

"You just chauffeur, or do you have other duties?"

"I do a little of this, a little of that, whatever the senator needs."

Out of habit, I jotted some notes in the old NYPD notebook I always carry with me.

Chauffeur—Clarence Washington, forty-plus, about six feet, two hundred pounds and well-muscled. Bodyguard for the family?

I sat back and enjoyed the ride. Each island has its own character and charm. Oahu is the most developed, and Honolulu is packed with high-rise hotels and commercial buildings.

On this day, a rainbow hovered over Manoa Valley. A few clouds dotted the Tiffany-blue sky without much threat of rain. I never care when it rains here. It rarely lasts long, and the heat and trades dry everything quickly, leaving only clean leaves and brilliant colors behind.

We were on Highway 72—the road surface torn up as usual—on the back side of Diamond Head. My grandkids want to hike the trail to the top. But I'm afraid with my bad leg, I'd never make it. Gerry could, though. She stays in good shape playing tennis and swimming. She also walks with a group from the college. *We'll have to come back with the kids.*

We turned off the main road just past Koko Head and

took a winding street to the top. It's an exclusive housing area. Some of the most expensive homes in the world are here. This is the area where Ferdinand Marcos stayed when he escaped from the Philippines.

The ornate wrought iron gates parted automatically as the limo pulled onto the long driveway. I noted a press van with satellite uplink and several other media cars stationed along the street outside. The main Hawaiian-style house sprawled on the bluff overlooking the sea.

Clarence led the way across the wide veranda to the massive entry.

On each side of the hall were large photos. One was of a very young couple I recognized as the senator and his wife. They faced each other before a Hawaiian sunset. Her hair flowed behind her, nearly reaching her waist. I assumed it was a wedding photo since they were both dressed in white with the long *maile* leis draped around their necks.

On the other side was another family photo, this one taken years earlier than the one I'd seen on TV. The adults in this photo leaned into each other and had protective arms around their young boys. I'd have guessed they were very close.

We continued through double doors with fancy etched glass panels and into the living room. We walked on past the curved stairway leading to the second floor and entered a small office.

"The senator will be right with you," Clarence said and turned, closing the door behind him.

The room had bookshelves on the walls and a large desk. Behind it, a picture window with curtains pulled back revealed a panoramic view of the ocean. The morning sun glinted off the breakers turning them molten silver.

I bet the sunsets are spectacular.

The door opened and the senator, wearing a conservative Hawaiian shirt, entered, followed by another man in a gray suit.

"Good of you to come," Senator Fowler said as he shook my hand and then settled into the leather chair behind his desk. I noticed the dark smudges beneath his eyes and the serious look on his face. "This is my legislative assistant, Bob Hillman. He'll be your main contact."

I took Mr. Hillman's hand. It was a cold, quick shake. With his index finger, Bob pushed his glasses back up the bridge of his nose, then indicated the chair in front of the desk. In contrast to the fit and tanned senator, Bob Hillman looked pale, small, and studious.

"Please be seated," he said, taking the side chair himself.

Senator Fowler opened a folder on the desk. It had my name on it.

"Very impressive record," he said. "Experienced detective with NYPD, then consultant with Maui County. Duke recommended you highly." He paused, and then looked up. "There are two rules. First, you will have free reign to do a thorough investigation. Anything you need, just ask Bob. Second, report whatever you discover to Bob or me first before taking it to the police. This is an election year and we can't afford any press leaks, no surprises. The media is already speculating about a conspiracy. I want the truth."

"That's why I'm here," I replied.

"Good, we wanted you because you're relatively unknown and shouldn't draw media attention. Try to keep it that way. The local police are on the case but haven't come up with anything so far." He looked a bit weary as he said it.

"Now," said the senator, rising from his chair, "I have another pressing meeting. Bob should be able to answer any questions you may have."

Another handshake and he was gone.

I took out my notebook, jotted a few items, and turned to Bob.

"The senator made the first announcement to the press a couple of days before the body was found. How did you first determine the boy was missing?"

"Philip was living with his girlfriend, Nicki Weaver, in a house in Hale'iwa. When he didn't return home from surfing Tuesday evening, she called to see if he was here. That was our first indication. The next day his car was found at Kaiaka Beach Park. It had been trashed. It's not a surfing beach. He would have had no reason to leave his car there."

"I'd like to talk to Nicki Weaver. But first, may I interview the rest of the family?"

"I'm sorry, Mrs. Fowler is so distraught over the death of her son, she was placed under sedation and is resting. Slade is away. He should return this evening."

"Well, maybe I should start with Ms. Weaver. But taking

the senator's limo to Hale'iwa might draw unwanted attention."

"We anticipated that and made arrangements for you. Clarence will drive you back to the airport. Mix with the crowd awhile. A rental car is waiting in stall number E-11. Here's the rental packet and key. A hotel reservation has been made in the name of Mr. A Jones at Turtle Bay."

Bob gave me Nicki's address and a little more information. Then he rose and shook my hand. "Good luck," he said.

Chapter 4: Watanabe

At the airport, I called the local detective assigned to the case, Masanobu Watanabe. Duke had given me his name and number before I left Maui. My years on the force had taught me that police work is a team effort. If the senator was expecting Magnum P.I., he would be disappointed.

"Aloha. This is Detective Watanabe," a pleasant but serious-sounding voice answered.

I introduced myself and briefed him on my morning meeting.

"Interesting," Watanabe commented. "The senator is right about one thing: the press is hounding us for information. Perhaps we should meet somewhere away from my office. I am currently at the substation on Waikiki Beach. Do you know the breakfast place *Eggs 'n Things* on Saratoga? It's always crowded, but I'm a friend of the owner and can get a table near the kitchen. With all the background noise, no one will overhear us. It's about a half-hour drive from the airport. I'll meet you there, say…eleven o'clock?"

I located a white Chevrolet Cobalt in space E-11. At the back gate, the attendant checked the rental agreement, returned it, and raised the crossing arm. I exited the lot and headed toward Waikiki via Nimitz Highway. I prefer that route to driving H1. It takes a few minutes longer, but it's much more scenic.

I hadn't been this way for several years and wanted to see the changes to the town. The Aloha Tower shopping area appeared to have been expanded again. Several *No Parking* signs had been added along Ala Moana Blvd., and I couldn't locate the big pineapple water tower that used to be near Hilo Hattie's.

I found a parking space on the street a couple of blocks from the restaurant. As I entered, a man seated at a two-person table in the far corner waved me over.

"Detective Watanabe?" I inquired.

"Mr. Jones. Duke's description of you is quite good." We shook hands. "Please be seated. And call me 'Masa.'"

In front of Masa sat a large platter holding the remains of a stack of strawberry pancakes, smothered in whipped cream, powdered sugar, and syrup. Next to it was a plate with two over-easy eggs and several strips of bacon awaiting consumption.

I picked up the menu. It contained an amazing number of items. I could hear Gerry's voice in my head, "*Agapé, remember your diet.*"

But she was on another island, I rationalized. I'd missed breakfast and it was almost lunchtime, so this could count as two meals. I opted for the Blueberry Crepes Suzettes.

Masa finished the rest of his meal and poured another cup of coffee.

Where does a small Asian man, maybe five-ten, one hundred fifty pounds, put all that food?

Watanabe looked serious. "So, the senator has brought in the big gun from NYPD." Then his face broke into a smile. "It is probably just as well. In the ten years he's been in state politics, we have investigated his suspicious activities on three different occasions. We have never been able to prove anything, though. I don't think he trusts us to *just* find his son's killer."

I wondered what he meant by 'suspicious activities.'

"Detective Duke got the lab reports back this morning," Masa continued. "He said to tell you the cause of death was the stab wound. The time of death was probably a few days before you found him but could not be accurately determined. Since it appeared the body had been in the water only a few hours at most, it must have been kept somewhere else. The corpse will be returned to Oahu sometime tomorrow."

He paused in thought then said, "I was surprised the younger son was the one who was killed. Everyone appeared to like Philip. He seemed a fine young man with a bright future in professional surfing. I also understand he was planning on moving to California to attend graduate school in the fall."

"Did he have any enemies? Anyone who might have threatened him?" I asked.

"The other surfers could have been jealous of how

quickly he gained prominence in the sport. But we haven't been able to identify anyone specific who had reason to harm him. We're still pursuing that angle."

I nodded and opened my notebook.

He continued, "Now the older brother, Slade, is a different story. A loner if there ever was one. He doesn't seem to have many friends, and we can't figure out what he does for a living. Of course, his family is very rich..."

He took a sip of coffee then went on. "Lately there appeared to be some friction in the Fowler household. The senator was pushing hard in the legislature for development of the North Shore. His wife and younger son were strongly against it. She's from Hale'iwa, you know. Her parents still live there. So did Philip."

I made quick notes of what he'd told me.

Masa moved closer to me and lowered his voice. "It's probably better if the local folks don't know you're working with the police. This North Shore Development issue is getting very serious. We've had to break up some protests by residents and make a few arrests. We are not very popular there right now."

"I'll keep that in mind," I said.

My crepes arrived. At Masa's suggestion, I augmented the sprinkled powdered sugar topping with the special guava syrup. Delicious!

He continued to talk while I eagerly consumed my meal, stopping only to write a few notes.

"So you met the senator this morning?" he asked.

"Yes, and his legislative assistant, Bob Hillman, too," I answered between bites.

"Hillman managed a very successful campaign for Senator Fowler's last reelection and then moved into the legislative assistant position. He's one smart operator. I'm told he can be a bit ruthless, though, especially where the senator's reputation is concerned."

Masa drained his cup. "I must get back to work," he stated as he stood and picked up the check. "This one is on me. You can get the next one. I'm sure we'll have another chat—soon."

As he turned to leave he paused. "One more bit of advice. If Mr. Hillman reserved your room, I'd check it for bugs."

I watched him pay and leave. My last half crepe seemed suddenly to have lost its attraction. I finished my coffee, left a tip for the waitress, and headed out the door and back toward the car. My cop intuition warned me I was investigating something more than just a murder. And Watanabe had all but told me I wouldn't get police backup in Hale'iwa. I'm sure Detective Duke wouldn't have recommended me if he'd expected danger. I'd better find out. *I'll call Duke on the way to Hale'iwa.*

I opened the rental car door, then stopped.

Hillman also ordered the Cobalt.

It took several minutes to locate the listening device under the dash near the firewall. An older model with audio only, no visual capability. I'd seen several like it during my

NYPD days. I left it in place.

Back on the street, I paused in front of an ABC store, acted as if I was browsing the cheap T-shirt bin, and glanced around. No one nearby. Good. I flipped open my cell and hit the speed dial.

Chapter 5: Reinforcements

"Well, Agapé, sounds like you've really gotten involved this time." Duke laughed.

I had just described the morning meetings and finding the listening device in the rental car. I was not in the mood for levity.

"Seriously," he continued, "I talked to Detective Watanabe this morning and agree it could be dangerous. I'll see what I can do to get you some backup in Hale'iwa. Officially, it's out of my jurisdiction, but maybe I can call in some favors. In the meantime, watch yourself."

"That's reassuring," I said, glancing up from the T-shirt bin to check around. No one in the ABC store paid any attention.

Duke ignored my sarcasm and continued, "Watanabe thinks this murder may be part of something much larger. He sees it as an opportunity to investigate the senator's activities. Had I known this earlier, I probably would have turned down the request," he apologized. "My few meetings with Senator

Fowler have always been cordial. He seemed like a man who was genuinely concerned for his family."

"I'll keep that in mind," I replied. "Don't know who planted the listening device or why. I'm heading to Hale'iwa to talk to Nicki Weaver, the girlfriend. I don't think whoever put the bug in my car knows I found it. I'll make a few innocuous calls from time to time so my listener feels useful."

"Good idea," Duke said. "If I call, just cough twice and I'll know we're being monitored. Good luck." He hung up.

The store clerk was giving me an inquisitive look. I must have loitered too long, and he was becoming suspicious.

Maybe I better act like a customer.

I selected a cheap tourist beach towel, aqua blue with floral border and "Hawaii" in large script, then grabbed a diet soda from the cooler and headed for the checkout. At least I could report to Gerry that I'd tried to stay on my diet. Maybe she wouldn't ask too many questions about breakfast.

Back in the car, I started the engine and headed out of town. It was a typical Honolulu morning, a bright blue sky dotted with puffy white clouds along the mountains, or as we say here, on the *mauka* side. The temperature, as usual, felt about seventy-eight degrees. It's nearly always seventy-eight degrees.

Passing over the Ala Wai Canal, I noticed several outriggers lined up along the bank. I remembered Kimo telling us bacteria levels in the canal had forced the clubs to move to Ke'ehi Lagoon last summer to avoid the pollution. Good to see the move was only temporary.

A thought occurred to me: *Hale'iwa has an outrigger club.* Kimo had mentioned it. To remain in shape for the upcoming events, I'd need to practice, and where better than Hale'iwa as I was staying on the North Shore?

As if on cue the phone rang, and I saw Kimo's name as I glanced at the display. Luckily there was a parking spot in the lot of a neighborhood market along McCully Street. I pulled in and answered.

"Agapé, my man," he began. "Uncle Duke tells me you're in need of a friendly face."

"You're right there," I replied and coughed twice.

Kimo had obviously gotten the message from Duke as his tone changed quickly. "Well, you should come back to Maui where people know and like you."

"I'd love nothing better than to be there. After all, I missed today's canoe practice. At this rate, I won't be in shape for the big race. Doesn't look like I'll be doing much paddling for a while," I confessed.

"You can't desert the team now. We need you for the Masters Fifty-five and Older competition."

"Maybe I could practice with a team here," I suggested. "Just to keep in shape, of course."

"I'll see what I can find out and get back to you. Take care," Kimo said as he hung up.

I set the cell on the seat and checked the mirror. As I pulled away from the curb, another car did the same.

Am I being followed? Keep your eyes open, Agapé.

A few blocks later, I made the left turn to enter H1

headed north. The other car didn't follow.

Within a few minutes, I had passed the airport, transitioned to H2, and started the climb across the island. I checked the rear view mirror often but didn't spot anyone tailing me. Whoever bugged the car might have also hidden a GPS tracker to follow the car's location. I'd already made one side trip to Waikiki, so thought I'd better stay on course to Hale'iwa, just in case.

I decided I'd stop at the Dole Plantation, a popular tourist spot, midway across the island. Several buses were parked in front. With all the ambient noise and confusion, I figured I could make some unmonitored calls. I entered the crowded store, mingled with the tourists, and purchased a pineapple smoothie. Most visitors stayed inside in the air conditioning or huddled on the shaded porch near the front door. I found an empty table outside at the very end of the lanai, far from the others, and dialed Kimo.

"Okay," I said without preamble, "why did you call earlier?"

"Uncle Duke said you needed a local contact."

"It sure might help. I understand the North Shore folks are suspicious of outsiders, particularly with all the controversy over the development proposals."

"That's what I thought, so I called my cousins Tommy and Toshi. They run a surf shop called Typhoon Tommy's in Hale'iwa. You won't have any trouble spotting it. It's on the main highway just before you get to the bridge near Matsumoto's. Stop by. They know you're coming."

"Thanks. Do you have relatives everywhere here in the islands?"

Kimo laughed. "Just about. Oh, by the way, their formal names are Tomohito and Toshihiro O'Malley."

It was my turn to laugh. I just love the Hawaiian melting pot. "Thanks, my friend. I owe you, as usual."

"No probs. Just take care of yourself, okay?"

"I'll do my best."

Time to make one more call. I wasn't looking forward to it. Gerry would not be happy about my staying on Oahu for several days. I was hoping to leave a short message, but she picked up on the second ring.

"Hello."

"Hi, gorgeous. How are you doing?"

"Just fine, sweetheart. When are you coming back?"

"It looks like I'll have to stay here a few days. These guys are really inexperienced. I'm afraid they'll miss something important if I'm not around to show them how it's done." It was just a little exaggeration. The local force wasn't used to these kinds of investigations. I could help them with the process. Of course, I hadn't exactly been asked to do that.

"Agapé, you're not getting too involved, are you? You're only advising, right?"

"Honey, I don't want to be involved any more than you want me to be." That wasn't a lie either. I was getting the feeling that this was bigger than just the murder of one surfer. I didn't know what the full story was, but I was afraid I wouldn't like it when I found out.

"You take care of yourself and watch your diet. Oh, and try to get some exercise." Gerry was always concerned about my health.

"Kimo is looking into the possibility of my practicing with an outrigger team while I'm here."

"I hope that works out. Now, be careful and come home soon."

"I'll do my best. Love ya. I'll call tonight when I get to the hotel."

"Okay. Love you, too. 'Bye."

The line went dead, and suddenly, more than anything, I wanted to be back on Maui with her, sitting on the lanai and enjoying the breeze.

I'd finished my smoothie and just gotten back on the road when the phone rang again. The theme from *Jaws* was getting nearly as annoying as the previous ring tone. I don't talk while driving. Fortunately there was almost no traffic, so I glanced at the display but didn't recognize the number. I pulled the car to the side of the road and stopped.

Maybe Gerry's right and I should get an earpiece.

"Jones here," I answered.

"Agapé, it's Raul."

"Raul, what a surprise."

"I was just talking to Kimo about the outrigger clubs on Oahu. I lived on the North Shore for a few years before moving to Maui. In fact, that's where I learned to paddle. He said you wanted to practice while you were there."

"Sure do. Got a name for me?" This was a conversation I

didn't mind my eavesdropper overhearing.

"Yeah. The president of the club when I was a member was Doc Schwenck. He's a good guy. And he's an even older geezer than I am!" He erupted into deep bellows of laughter. I joined him. "I think he's still a member of the club in Hale'iwa. I'll give you his phone number."

I pulled out my notebook and jotted it down. "Thanks, man, I owe you one."

Raul's voice became serious as he said, "Take care and come back soon." I wondered how much Kimo had told him.

"That's my plan. Thanks again for your help."

"It's nothing. I'm protecting my own interests since you sit behind me." He chuckled again. "See you soon." The line went dead.

I debated calling Doc as long as I was off the road but decided to wait until I reached Hale'iwa. I'd be there in about twenty minutes and didn't know what awaited me.

Chapter 6: Typhoon Tommy

The quiet little town of Hale'iwa was a delightful change from the hurried activity of Waikiki and the big city of Honolulu. It's the gateway to the North Shore. Even though the town had grown some, nothing much had changed since my previous visit.

Bob Hillman had given me Nicki Weaver's address and directions, so I decided to start with her. She lived in the older part of town near the harbor. Unlike the huge mansions in Hawai'i Kai, this area featured small shacks, mobile homes, lots of rusting vehicles, and evidence of a more relaxed lifestyle.

I followed directions and found myself in front of a little green house. This one had fresh paint and crisp white curtains in the windows.

I eased out of the car, thankful to move my bad leg after all the driving. I still have a bullet in it from my last assignment on the force. The injury led to my retirement and left me with a limp. If I do my exercises and don't sit in one spot for long without moving, it doesn't cause me much pain. However, it had been a long drive from the city, even with the stop on the way. I was feeling a bit stiff.

As I walked to the door, I discreetly cased the neighborhood. The street was deserted except for an elderly lady in a muumuu and floppy hat pruning roses next door, and a lone parked car at the far end of the block. Dark tinted windows prevented me from seeing inside.

I knocked several times, to no answer.

"She's not home yet," a firm voice interrupted from nearby. The neighbor set down her pruning shears and peered up at me from under her hat. "You one of those news people? Sure don't look like one."

"No," I replied, "just someone who needs to talk with Nicki. You wouldn't know when she'll be back?" I always found it better to use the person's name. It sounded friendlier and tended to dilute suspicions.

"I sure hope you're not one of those nosy reporters. Too many of them sniffin' around here lately." She gave me an appraising stare, then seemed to decide I was okay. "She should be finishing her shift at Schofield Clinic about now. Usually gets home around three. Say, if you're a friend, shouldn't you know that?"

"We have a mutual acquaintance who asked me to get in touch," I replied. "I'll check back later when she's home." I quickly returned to my car. I didn't want to arouse any more curiosity.

As I drove away, I breathed a little easier when the

parked car I'd seen earlier didn't follow.

Since Nicki wasn't available, I decided to visit Typhoon Tommy's surf shop. It was right where Kimo had said. I pulled the rental car into the last available space in the small dirt lot at the side. The wall was painted with a two-story-high mural of a tubing Banzai Pipeline wave. At one end, the front half of a surfboard protruded from the wall. Several tourists alternately stood on the board and took pictures of each other. With the painted wave backdrop and much imagination, it might almost appear as if one were actually riding a giant wave. *Must make great snapshots to send to the relatives back in Minnesota*, I mused.

I entered the dimly-lit shop. Pale blue-green light entered through the painted-over second floor windows. Clothing racks and display shelves piled with sale items crowded narrow aisles. Along one wall stood a row of new surfboards arranged by length, the shortest near the front and the big ones at the rear. In an alcove in the back, used boards of varying size and condition were less formally clustered.

To one side, a glass display counter held surf videos, DVDs, underwater watches, wax, and other necessary paraphernalia. On top was an old-fashioned cash register. Behind the counter sat a short, stocky Asian-Hawaiian with black curly hair and beard. He reminded me a little of Brutus (or was it Bluto?) from the old Popeye cartoons.

"I'm looking for Tommy," I began.

He paused and looked me over. "Then you're in the right place," he finally answered.

I held out my hand. "I'm Agapé Jones. Kimo may have told you about me."

"Sure did. Why don't we go somewhere a little less public? Follow me."

Several people wandered about the shop, so I thought his suggestion a wise one. I followed him around the counter and through a small door into an adjoining office.

"Toshi, could you man the counter for a few minutes?"

This must be his brother, but there's certainly little resemblance. Toshi looked more Asian and less Hawaiian. He was even shorter than Tommy, maybe five-four, very thin, and clean-shaven with a mop of straight, thick, ebony hair.

"Sure, brudda," he said as he left.

The office was tiny and overflowed with paper. A strong wind or small earthquake would have caused an avalanche. I wondered how they ever found anything. Tommy swept a stack off an old folding chair and onto the floor.

"Have a seat," he offered. He dumped another pile on top of the first, clearing a corner of the old wooden desk where he perched. "Kimo said you were in need of a friend in the neighborhood."

"You're right about that." I was grateful, once again, that Kimo had relatives throughout the islands. "What did he tell you?"

"Said you were investigating Flip's death, sort of undercover."

"That's right. I'd like to keep a low profile while I'm here."

He nodded. "Good idea. There's lots of tension at the moment. The locals think the cops are in bed with the North Shore developers. And there have been all the reporters with their cameras and microphones. Our little town hasn't been the same. The cops and the press even questioned me."

"What did you tell them?" I took out my trusty notebook and poised my pencil for writing.

"I told them the same thing I'd tell you." He sounded a little defensive. "Flip was a good guy—one of the best. He was polite, friendly, and everybody liked him. He was also one of the top surfers on the North Shore. He had everything going for him."

"Can you think of anyone who might have been threatened by him? Anyone who resented him?"

"Well, Jake Bradley's been the spokesman and poster boy for Liquid Excitement Surfboards. He's the owner and designer. Still works along with the other guys. But he's getting older and can't keep up with the younger kids on the waves. It was his decision to add Flip to the ads. Seems like he was okay with it, but you never know."

"Philip was doing ads for them?"

"Yeah. He did the first one with Jake after he won a local contest on one of their boards." He rifled around a nearby stack and fished out a magazine. Opening it to a full-page ad, he shoved it toward me. The Liquid Excitement logo was spread across the top. On the right-hand side was a picture of Philip Fowler standing proudly next to a board. On the left-hand side was another older guy with his. The headline said,

Ride with the Best—Liquid Excitement.

"I notice you carry that brand," I observed.

"We were the exclusive distributor for about eight years. Since Flip won the Masters, they've lined up other retailers and started selling overseas. The shop's out back."

"It is?"

"Yeah. They rent a big metal warehouse. Used to be where sugar cane and pineapple were stored before being shipped to the mainland. It's not used for that any more since there's less grown here. United Shipping offered it for lease about the same time the guys started making boards."

"The guys?"

"Liquid Excitement was started by a small group of surfers. Along with Jake, Winston Wackenhut, known as 'Wacko' around here, is the head shaper. Jim Whyte was the glasser until his stroke a few months ago. Now there's a new guy named Cho. Don't know much about him. Keeps to himself. Jamie Aiku-Howe is the sander. I think his family helped bankroll the start-up. Slade Fowler was involved in some way, too. Probably with finances."

"Would any of them have resented Philip's success?" It didn't seem likely, but who knew what their personal dynamics were?

Tommy seemed to give the question serious thought before he answered. "Wacko was a promising pro surfer in his teens. Then he got involved with booze and drugs. Seems as though he lost a few too many brain cells. But he's a good shaper."

"Do you think he might have been jealous of Philip?"

"Maybe. He's kind of a nutcase. But he seems pretty harmless."

"What about the other one, uh..." I had to check my notes for the name. "Jamie?"

"Jamie was a reckless kid. Had real talent but knew no fear. A few years ago, he decided to go out at Waimea on a big day. The sets were closing out and the rest of the guys told him it was too dangerous, but he didn't listen."

He paused for a second, and I wondered why. Then he took a deep breath and continued. "He was too late taking off on the biggest wave of the day. Went over the falls and was slammed against the bottom. The wave carried him toward the beach. The North Shore Lifeguards dragged him in. They got him breathing, but his back was broken."

"How bad was it?"

"He's in a chair. Still has the use of his arms, though."

Tommy looked sad and shook his head. "Kid came from a rich family. Since the accident, they've given him everything he wanted. Guilt, maybe. They were off-island when it happened."

"Do you know his family?"

"Not really. Jamie was raised by nannies and caretakers. But after he was paralyzed, his parents seemed to be trying to make up for lost time. Got him the best racing and power chairs made. Kid has several. He has a boat, too. Custom-rigged for his wheelchair."

"Are his parents more involved now?"

Tommy looked even sadder, if that were possible. "Nope. It's like they spend money on stuff to avoid being with him."

"You think he might have resented Philip? After all, he was young and healthy and doing everything Jamie couldn't."

"I don't know. He seems to be trying to get his folks' attention and doesn't seem to care much about what anyone else is doing. Matter of fact, building boards is the only thing that keeps him connected to the local surfing crowd." He paused. "Spends a lot of time on his boat fishing. But I haven't seen many fish." Then he laughed.

"Thanks. Maybe you could introduce me. I have a grandson who wants to surf. I'd like to learn more about how the boards are made and what he would need. It could be a nice Christmas gift."

"Sure, man. Any time."

"Oh, one more thing. I'm going to try to spend some time paddling with the local canoe club. It seems like a good cover story for my being here. A member of our team on Maui gave me the number for Doc Schwenck. Told me to call him. Is there anything I should know?" I figured it would be better to be prepared in case he was affiliated with any of the local factions.

Tommy grinned. "Doc's a good guy. Big-time plastic surgeon, one of the best in the world. Belongs to a group called *Beyond Our Borders*. Volunteers his time going to foreign countries to help disfigured kids. Doesn't charge, either."

"I understand he's the president of the local club."

"Yeah. He and his wife, Grace, moved here about twenty years ago. He was gone a lot between his practice at Queens Hospital in Honolulu and his volunteer travel. Came home one day and found Gracie dead. Heart attack. They were married for forty-seven years. Losing her nearly killed Doc."

I thought for a second how I'd feel if I lost Gerry. Life wouldn't have as much meaning, that's for sure.

"He stopped going out or seeing anybody. Gave up his practice and volunteer work, too. Then some friends invited him to a party. He didn't want to go, but they pressured him 'til he said yes. Good thing he went 'cause he met Naomi there."

"Who's Naomi?" I didn't know where this story was leading, but I figured he'd get to it eventually. In Hawaii, people love to 'talk story.' Drawing out the details is part of a cultural tradition. Asking them to get to the point is useless once they get started.

"She was the wife of Johnny Mitchell. Maybe you heard about him. Made plenty of money in the stock market. Moved here to get away from the bustle of the mainland and hang loose. Built a big house just this side of Waimea. Great view.

"Started paddling with the North Shore Canoe Club and became the center of local society. But about a year later, Johnny was driving back from Turtle Bay alone. As he came around the bend at the north end of the Waimea Bay, a truckload of drunken teenagers took the curve too fast, crossed over the centerline, and creamed his little sports car."

"Hmmm." I made a sound to let him know I hadn't dozed off.

"Naomi was really lost. She had lots of money but wasn't used to having to make decisions. She went to the same party as Doc, and they met. Best thing that could have happened. They helped each other start living again."

"Great story—" I began.

"She got Doc to join the club. He loved paddling. Been doing it ever since. Married Naomi about five years ago. She's a lot younger, but they're good together. You'll meet her."

"Is there anyone else in the club I should know about? I wouldn't want to get mixed up in any local battles."

Tommy thought for a moment. "Terry Ventura works for Senator Fowler. He's an aide or clerk or something. Don't know him too well. Most of the others are retired or don't get involved in the local politics. Can't think of anyone you need to worry about."

I shook his hand. "Well, thanks for everything. I'll see you soon."

Nicki should be home by now.

Chapter 7: Nicki

As I drove onto the street, I noticed that the car with the tinted windows was still there, but in a different location. *Well, it isn't abandoned.*

The little lady next door had apparently finished her pruning since she wasn't in her yard. However, I thought I saw the curtains move a little as I pulled up in front of Nicki's house. It could have been the breeze, but I suspected the neighbor had been waiting for me to return and was checking.

This time a voice answered my second knock. "Coming." The door opened to reveal a small dark-haired young woman. (I actually thought 'girl,' but I knew about how old she was.)

"Yes?" she said, eyeing me a bit suspiciously.

"I hate to bother you, Miss Weaver, but I'd like to speak with you if I may."

"What about?" She looked even more wary.

"Well, I was one of the people who found Philip's body on Maui..."

"Oh." I watched her dark eyes fill, but they didn't overflow.

"I'm sorry to bring up something this painful for you, but I'd like to talk with you about it." I chose my words carefully. If my car was bugged, I suspected her house might be, too.

"I don't know if I..." she began.

"Please. I've been haunted by the incident, and learning a bit more about Philip might help me come to terms with everything. He was such a young man with his whole life ahead of him. I keep wishing I'd known him."

"I guess I get that," she conceded.

"Listen, if you're hungry, I'd like to buy you dinner." It would get us out of the house and away from my car. That might be the best way to talk candidly—unless we were followed.

"I don't think so. I don't even know who you are."

"I'm sorry. My name is Agapé Jones. I'm retired from the NYPD and living on Maui." I pulled my NYPD commemorative shield from my pocket where I always keep it. I'd feel naked without it.

She nodded.

"My racing team from Kihei Canoe Club was practicing for the Molokai race when we spotted Philip's body. If you'd like to check, Tommy O'Malley at Typhoon Tommy's can vouch for me. His cousin Kimo is one of my rowing partners."

"Well, I guess. As long as we're somewhere public." She still looked apprehensive.

"Since you live here, where would you suggest?"

She actually tried to smile. "Would you like to eat the best burger on Oahu? I didn't get lunch, and I've been thinking about one all afternoon."

I was certain Gerry wouldn't approve, but it was in the line of duty, after all. "That sounds good to me."

"If you'd just wait a minute, I'll be right with you."

I knew she was still uncomfortable, so I volunteered to wait in the car.

After a few minutes, she joined me.

"Tommy says you're okay," she said as she settled on the passenger side and hooked her seat belt.

"I'm glad you checked. I have a couple of granddaughters about your age. I sure wouldn't want them getting into a car with a stranger."

I was rewarded with another slight smile.

"Where to?" I asked.

"Back to Kam Highway and turn right. It'll be on your left a few blocks down."

"So they make the best burgers in the area?"

"No, not just in the area. The Kua 'Aina Sandwich Shop makes the best burgers on Oahu, maybe in the whole world. It's been rated number one here for years, and I agree."

"Well, that's a good enough recommendation for me." It felt as though I were with one of my son Martin's girls, Tanisha and Lauren. They don't come to visit as often as my grandson, Malcolm, and I miss them.

She pointed the way. It wasn't far. After parking, I went

around to the passenger door to open it for her. She seemed surprised but took the hand I offered to help her out.

The place was crowded and we had to wait in line. That gave us a chance to look at the choices posted above the counter. There were too many, and they all sounded good. I asked her to order for us.

We finally reached the counter.

"Two one-third-pound bacon cheeseburgers with grilled onions." She looked at me to see if that was okay.

I wouldn't be kissing Gerry tonight, so I nodded my approval.

"And we'll split an order of shoestring fries."

Gerry couldn't object too much. It wasn't a full order.

"Drinks?" asked the gal behind the counter.

"Diet Coke for me," I said.

"Make that two Diet Cokes," Nicki told the girl.

I looked around and noticed a couple getting up from a small table in the corner. I pointed, and Nicki headed in that direction while I paid and waited for our drinks.

I surveyed the room. No one seemed to pay any attention to us. The tables nearest the one where Nicki sat had been occupied when we came in. I thought we were probably secure.

I set the two drinks on the table and took a chair.

"If these burgers taste as good as they smell, you could be right about their rating."

She smiled with her mouth, but her eyes didn't share the emotion. It pleased me to be able to make her a little happier. I was sure it hadn't happened often in the last few days.

Our order arrived quickly, including a huge basket of fries. Each burger was accompanied by a large dill pickle wedge. She offered me hers. I hate to see good food go to waste, so...

As we ate the best burgers in all of Oahu, perhaps in the whole world, I began. "Tell me about Philip. He was obviously very handsome, and from what I've been able to discover, very smart, too."

"When I first saw him at UH, the sun was shining on his hair and he looked like he was wearing a halo. I thought he was the most beautiful guy I'd ever seen."

"You rarely hear 'beautiful' used in connection with a male."

"I know, but it's how I saw him. I've seen pictures of Michelangelo's David, and Phil was even more impressive."

"So you two met at the university?"

"Yes. I was in the nursing program, and he was studying oceanography. He loved the sea, everything about it. He used to say he felt more at home in the water than on land."

"So that's why he took up surfing?"

She tried to smile again. "Mr. Jones, every little kid in Hawaii takes up surfing. Most of them go out with their parents before they can walk. Phil was just better than the others." There was a definite hint of pride in her voice.

"Was he planning a career in the sport?"

"No. Oh, he loved doing it, but he wasn't really very competitive."

That confused me and it must have shown on my face.

"He only wanted to be the best he could be. He saw himself as his only rival. I think that's why the rest of the pros liked him."

"But didn't some of the others resent his ability? I'm sure most of them were competing against him."

"Actually, he helped anyone who needed it. During last year's Xcel Pro Contest at Sunset Beach, he bailed on the wave of the day to avoid hitting a fellow surfer. He always said, 'Another wave with my name on it will come along.'" She choked slightly, and I assumed she'd realized that there were no more waves with Philip's name on them.

"What was your relationship with Philip like?" This was the information I really needed.

She closed her eyes and took a deep breath. Then she looked straight at me. "I adored Phil from the moment I saw him. Do you believe in love at first sight?"

It happened I did, since I had loved Gerry the instant she came through my front door. She was just a kid and my sister's friend at the time. For the next couple of years, I tried to forget her, but it was impossible. We've been married for over forty years now, and I can't imagine life without her.

I just answered, "Yes."

"Well, for me that's what it was."

"Did Philip feel the same way?"

"Not right away. As a matter of fact, he was pretty clueless. I asked around and discovered he didn't have a girlfriend. He was more interested in studying. His older brother, Slade, had a very different reputation when it came to females. But Phil was dedicated to his education."

"So how did you two get together?"

"There was a big end-of-summer beach party. I went with my girlfriends. Phil was already there trying out the waves when we arrived. I managed to walk by him as he came out of the water and asked him to join us. Since we had food..."

I chuckled and said, "We men are pretty easy to convince when there's a meal involved."

"Well, Phil was. We talked and talked that evening, and he called the next day. We became a couple pretty quickly."

"I understand you were engaged." Bob Hillman had told me during my briefing.

She looked sad again. "We were. Last Christmas he gave me a ring that had belonged to his grandmother. It was very sweet, and I assumed we'd be married when he graduated. But he changed all that."

"How?"

"He said he was going to do his graduate work at Scripps in California."

"Why was that a problem?" I assumed that young people were pretty transient these days.

"I'm the head nurse in the clinic at Schofield, a position which usually goes only to seasoned professionals. I was promoted after just one year of actual experience."

"How did that happen?"

"The clinic serves the military families on this part of the island. Since Pearl is one of the most desirable duty locations, people come and go. The previous director had been there for four years. The one before him left after two. The clinic's management wanted to hire someone who was civilian and would stay. Since I graduated at the top of my class, I was accepted."

"So you felt you couldn't leave your job?"

"Yes, and no. It was more than that." She paused. "Both Phil and I come from *ali'i* families. Are you familiar with what that means?"

"Yes." The *ali'i* were Hawaiian royalty. Had the monarchy not been overthrown by the Americans, one of them might very well be the ruler of these islands."

"I was raised to take my heritage very seriously. So was Phil. Our families were delighted to see the two of us engaged. Slade used to call Phil his '*haole* brother' because of his fair complexion and blond hair. But Phil was the brother more connected to his native roots, even though Slade looks more Hawaiian."

"Why would that be a problem?"

"It's a little complicated. Phil's dad, Senator Fowler, comes from a long line of California politicians. One was Attorney General, and several others served as state senators and representatives. The senator came to Hawaii originally to make a name for himself, on his own, and to get away from the pressure in California. Phil's mother and I were afraid that if he went there, his mainland family would swallow him up."

"I guess I still don't understand." It didn't sound like a big deal to me.

"Phil's Fowler grandparents have a lot of political clout

there. They're still angry that their son is not an elected official in their area of influence. Slade, the heir apparent, was being groomed for the family legacy, but he turned out to be a disappointment. That left Phil."

"Let's see if I understand. You were afraid that if Philip left Hawaii, he wouldn't come back?"

"Precisely. And I told him so. As a matter of fact, we argued about it the night before he disappeared, and I told him I'd give the ring back." She began to cry. "Maybe if I hadn't..." She looked down at the ring on her finger.

I didn't know what to say.

Was she angry enough to have been involved with Philip's death? She doesn't seem angry now, but Philip's dead. She isn't a large person. Could she have inflicted the wound I saw? I doubt it. Yet it sounds as though she felt betrayed. And betrayal can lead to violence.

I added her name to my notebook.

Suspects:
Other surfers?

"I'm sorry," she sniffled.

"I understand," I replied. "This has been tough for you." I'd have been more surprised if she hadn't been upset.

She sat up straight and took a sip of her soda. There was still half a basket of fries left, although we had done a pretty good job of reducing it. She'd only eaten half her burger.

"Looks like you need a container to take that home," I

observed and got up to go to the counter.

When I returned, she'd stopped crying. She was silent as she boxed the remainder of her sandwich.

"Thanks for sharing your story with me. I feel as though I know Philip a little better," I said.

She gave me that direct look again. "Thank you for letting me talk about the Phil I knew and loved."

My cell phone rang. She raised an eyebrow as the theme from *Jaws* came out of my pocket. "Excuse me," I said to her as I answered.

"Jones here."

"Agapé, it's Duke. Can you talk?"

"Not right now, but I'll call you back in a little while."

"I'll be waiting." He hung up.

"I'm sorry…" I began.

"No, it's all right," she said as she stood and collected her leftovers.

"Are you ready to go?"

"Yes, thanks."

"You were right. That may have been one of the best burgers I ever ate."

She gave me another of her attempts to smile.

We were both silent on the short ride. I thanked her again as I helped her out of the car. She nodded, and I watched her enter her house.

As I drove away, the light came on in the house next door. I also noticed the car with the tinted windows was gone.

But my first priority was to find out what Duke wanted.

Chapter 8: Making Plans

I couldn't make a secure call from inside my car, so I decided Hale'iwa Ali'i Beach Park might be okay. It was outdoors, and I could observe all the activity from the rise in the middle.

I went back to Hale'iwa Road, turned into the park, and drove to the far end of the lot. I'd watched to be certain I wasn't being followed. I was afraid I was becoming a bit paranoid, but the bug in the car made me extra cautious.

I eased out of the seat, locked the door, and strolled toward the beach. The waves were small, and the onshore wind had roughened the ocean's surface. No surfers were in the water, although several families lounged on the warm sand and a group of young children was building a sand castle along the shore.

I turned to the right and crossed a low bluff overlooking the small boat harbor. The slips were mostly filled. Two large catamarans were tied along the wharf near the commercial fishing boats. I particularly noted one large yacht which didn't fit into a slip and was tied up across the end of the dock. It looked out of place somehow. There were also several racing boats and other pleasure craft—maybe three dozen in all.

I continued to a spot where I could be sure no one was close enough to hear my conversation, then hit the speed dial for Duke.

"Agapé here," I announced when he answered. "What's up?"

"I know Watanabe told you that the cause of death was a wound to the chest, probably from a knife."

"Yes, he did."

"He probably also told you about some strange particles we found deep in the nostrils and ear canals." Masa hadn't mentioned this. I wondered why, but didn't say anything to Duke.

He continued, "We're testing to identify the substance. I'll let you know when we get the results."

"Anything on the blood and tox panels? I was just talking to his girlfriend, Nicki Weaver. She's the head nurse at the Schofield Clinic and has access to drugs."

"Those tests will take a little longer, too. We're hoping to have all the answers tomorrow…or the next day."

"Any word on when the body will be released?" I wondered how much time I'd have before the attention moved to Oahu.

"The coroner and ME said they won't release the body until the test results are back. We've heard from the family that they want him as soon as possible. We also heard there's some disagreement as to what happens after that."

"What are they arguing about?" I thought it best to know where the factions were positioned.

"I guess the mainland relatives want Philip buried in California and the Hawaiian ones want him cremated. They feel obligated to observe the local cultural traditions."

"What do you mean?"

"He's of royal Hawaiian ancestry. He was also a surfer. It'll be a big deal. The body will be cremated and the ashes spread at sea."

"That doesn't sound like a big deal to me."

"Oh, it will be. They'll hold a memorial service at that big stone church in downtown Honolulu where the choir sings in Hawaiian."

"I think I know the one you're talking about." I'd listened to the choir on the radio several times and always wanted to hear them in person.

"Then, all the family will board a catamaran yacht. A calabash with the ashes will be onboard. Surfers on their boards and other canoes will accompany it beyond the surf line. There'll be chanting and singing and the ashes will be spread. The *ali'i* ceremony is filled with tradition, and so is the surfer one. Combining them will be a *huge* deal."

"Will the press cover it?"

"Without a doubt. It'll be all over the news. Dad's a prominent politician, Mom is *ali'i,* and the kid was a champion surfer. The place'll be crawling with reporters."

"Guess I'd better question the key people before that if I

want to remain inconspicuous." I didn't intend to become part of the story.

. "You'd better work fast then, my friend. If I hear something, I'll call. And if you need anything, do the same."

"Thanks. I'll keep that in mind."

"And, Agapé, I'm sorry I put you in this mess. Had I known…

"It's okay. I agreed to come."

"Well, watch your back."

"I intend to."

I hung up and looked around again. Still no sign of anyone nearby. One family had packed up and was heading back to their car. The rest of those remaining seemed to be enjoying the waning afternoon.

I looked at my watch. *Maybe I should check into the hotel. If I don't do it soon, whoever's tracking my movements might wonder.*

From the park, it was only about ten miles up to Turtle Bay, but the drive took closer to twenty minutes because of the single lane in each direction and the surfers trying for a late afternoon on the waves.

When I arrived at the hotel and pulled up in front, I was informed my car would be valet parked. I thought it a little strange. Perhaps this was simply hotel courtesy, or maybe they were waiting for me.

Check-in went as I had expected—without incident. But I was surprised that my 'room' was not in the hotel proper. I followed a bellman outside to one of the beach cottages. These were luxury suites, two or three to a building.

We entered, and I stood facing a wall of windows looking out on the ocean. We were in the bedroom area, which was raised two steps above the sitting room.

After I tipped the bellman, I began a sweep for listening devices.

The place was tastefully—and expensively—furnished. Besides the king-size bed covered with a silky Hawaiian print spread, the 'bedroom' contained a large dresser, an armoire, two nightstands, and two chairs with upholstered Hawaiian print cushions. The furniture looked as though it might have been koa wood, Gerry's favorite. I knew what it cost. That's why we don't have any furniture made of it.

I scanned for cameras. There weren't any, but I easily located the bug behind one nightstand.

Off to the side were a large dressing room and a luxurious bath. It had a skylight. There were two sinks, a walk-in closet, and the tub was a whirlpool. The way the room was arranged, I could sit in the tub and watch the waves breaking. *Now this is luxury.* The only thing not there was my beautiful bride. I suddenly missed her very much.

I moved down the two steps to the lower level. On one side were a table and four chairs in that same glowing wood. Along the wall was a mini-kitchen with a small refrigerator, sink, coffee maker, and cabinets, which I assumed held dishes.

On the other side of this room were a desk, a sofa, two chairs, end tables with lamps, and a large glass-topped coffee table. I was surprised to discover another bug cleverly hidden under the carved center of the coffee table base.

From the sitting room, sliding doors led to a lanai, much like ours at home, only larger. The table, chairs, and two lounges were better quality than our plastic ones.

Turning to go back inside, I noticed the artwork. On the wall behind the sofa was what appeared to be an original oil painting of a Hawaiian seascape. I carefully felt around the frame but found nothing. The picture was permanently fastened to the wall. I glanced at the signature and was surprised to see it looked like 'Schwenck.' *Doc maybe?*

There was another large painting above the bed. I assured myself there were no electronics around that one, too. This seascape looked identical to the view from this room and had the same signature.

I hadn't located any cameras. Guess they didn't care what I looked like. Or maybe they already knew. But the transmitters were tiny and of a newer technology than the one in my car.

I began to unpack. It looked as though I would be here a few days, at least. Then I took my toiletries into the bathroom. As I set them down, I dropped an aspirin bottle which rolled under the toilet. I admit I was surprised to look up and see another of the little transmitters mounted on the wall behind it. *Lucky drop*, I thought.

I decided to call Doc since he was already on my mind. I figured we wouldn't discuss anything I'd mind anyone else hearing. He answered on the first ring.

"Hello, this is Agapé Jones. Maybe Raul Garcia mentioned me."

"Great! I've been expecting your call. You're the answer

to our prayers. We're one paddler short since a regular is on the Mainland and our sub was called away on a family emergency. Raul said you needed to stay in practice." He chuckled. "I used to sit behind him myself. He's a perfectionist and expects everyone else to be as good as he is."

"Yeah, but he's a great paddler."

"One of the best. Would you be able to join us at dawn tomorrow? A couple of the guys have to work, so we practice early."

"My team does too. Exactly what time is 'early'?"

"Six a.m. We paddle out at that time, so you should plan on getting there before then."

"Where is 'there'?"

"Where are you staying?"

"Turtle Bay."

"Did you drive from Hale'iwa?"

"Yes." I realized that I could have taken the longer drive through Kailua.

"Okay, take the highway back to Hale'iwa. We're on the right-hand side, just before you get to the bridge."

"I think I can find it."

"Good. We'll see you in the morning."

We hung up before I thought to ask him about the paintings. But I figured I could find out tomorrow.

I wasn't very hungry. I still felt comfortable from the burger at lunch. But a snack sounded good, so I checked the menu on the desk. Everything the restaurant was serving was more than I wanted. I did notice that they had *pupus* by the pool all day. That sounded better.

It was a nice walk over to the pool, and I was ready to eat when I arrived. I ordered a large iced tea. I couldn't allow alcohol to dull my instincts. The Blue Hawaiis would have to wait until I could mix them up special to celebrate my homecoming.

I'm pretty adventurous when it comes to food. The selection looked mouthwatering. I enjoyed the *ahi poke*, Hawaiian spareribs, and macadamia nut hummus. But the coconut-battered shrimp were the best. I sat down near the pool and watched the sunset. I hoped Gerry was enjoying the same view.

I missed her so much, I went back to the room to call home. I didn't mind too much if the calls to Doc and Gerry were overheard.

"Hi, sugar," I said. "I miss you."

"Honey, I miss you too." She sounded a little down.

"I may be here for a couple more days. They haven't released the body yet, and I need to help the locals with some legwork."

"I understand, but I don't have to like it."

"I didn't say I liked it. I don't. But one good thing is that a friend of Raul's invited me to paddle with his team tomorrow morning."

"I'm glad you're keeping in shape while you're there."

"I just wish you were here with me. You should see this place. It has a whirlpool tub. We could sit in it and watch the ocean."

"You're joking, aren't you?"

"No. I'll try to take some pictures for you."

"Good. I wish I could get over there to join you, but this special summer class I'm teaching is moving very quickly. I can't afford a day off. Please take care of yourself and hurry home. You know I won't sleep well without you here snoring next to me."

"No one wants to finish this more quickly than I do because I don't sleep well alone either."

"Love you, honey."

"Love you, too. See you soon. 'Bye."

I was thankful she hadn't asked about my diet. I didn't want to have to explain breakfast or lunch.

It wasn't quite time for bed, so I turned on the TV I discovered in the armoire and watched a mindless program. Then I set my alarm and turned out the light. Dawn would come early.

Chapter 9: Outrigger Morning

I awoke to an unfamiliar sound. It took a few seconds to realize I wasn't back home on Maui and to locate the clock on the nightstand to silence the buzz.

The red numbers on the clock read four-thirty. *Boy, that's early,* I thought as I began my morning physical therapy. My daily routine, started at the insistence of my doctor following the bullet wound that ended my career, consisted of two sets of thirty leg lifts on my back, stomach, and both sides. Of course, I hadn't brought my five-pound leg weights with me, so today's exercise wouldn't be quite as beneficial.

I finished my PT, showered, slipped on my Kihei Canoe Club T-shirt, and pulled my cargo shorts on over a pair of swim trunks. No time for breakfast if I wanted to meet Doc before five-thirty.

The sun slowly brightened the sky in the rearview mirror as I navigated Kam Highway back toward Hale'iwa. Several surfers were already in the water at Sunset Beach. Passing the big church tower and rounding Waimea Bay, I remembered Tommy's story of the accident that took the life of Doc's wife's first husband.

I turned off the highway just before the iron bridge, parked, and stowed my shorts in the trunk. I tied the car key to the drawstring of my swim trunks. Several outriggers were pulled up on the sand nearby. A young man stood near one of the canoes. I could tell he was serious. His paddle, *hoe* in Hawaiian, shaft down, rested against the side of the craft. Only a novice paddler stuck the blade or *laulau* of the paddle in the sand. He gave me an inquisitive, almost defensive, look as I approached.

"Hi. I'm Agapé Jones from the Kihei Canoe Club on Maui," I said, extending my hand. "Doc Schwenck invited me to join the paddle this morning."

His serious expression softened to a broad smile and he reached for my hand in a friendly shake.

"I'm Terry," he said. "There's an extra *hoe* in the box by the palm. I think it's about your size. The others should be here shortly."

"Nice to meet you, Terry," I replied, thinking, *Terry. Wasn't that the name Tommy mentioned as the aide to Senator Fowler? Hmmm, I might have a few questions for him.*

I was about to speak when a late model SUV pulled up and three people exited. The driver was an elderly but very fit-looking man with gray, thinning hair and neatly-trimmed beard. *Must be Doc.* The front seat passenger was an equally fit but appreciably younger female with blond hair, dark tan, and dazzling smile. The third member was a young islander. Even through his T-shirt, I could make out extremely well-developed shoulder muscles. These were serious paddlers.

"You must be Agapé Jones," the older man said as the trio approached. "Raul gave you a good recommendation." I gripped his offered hand. "This is my wife, Naomi, and Keola, our number-one paddle. As soon as Barbara gets here, we'll be on our way. You're sitting in for Georgia today; she's off island for the next two weeks. I hope you can be with us for a while. Our team needs practice to be ready for the state championships in August. We're competing in the Experienced Mixed Team category."

Barbara arrived on her bicycle and locked it to a tree, while I retrieved a *hoe* from the equipment box.

We began our practice session by forming a circle on the sand and performing the *E Ala E*, the Hawaiian traditional chant to welcome the rising sun:

E ALA E
E ALA E
KA LAI I KA HIKINA
Awake, the sun is in the east
I KA MOANA
KA MOANA HOU HONU
At the ocean, the deep ocean
PI`I KA LEWA
KA LEWA NU`U
Climb to the heavens, highest heaven
I KA HIKINA
AE A KALA
E ALA E
In the east, there is the sun, arise, awake

I was familiar with the ritual and knew the words, since we do the same back on Maui. I closed my eyes and felt at home.

"You take third paddle, behind Barbara," Doc directed as we lined up to move the big outrigger to the water's edge.

Today was to be a short sprint up to Keālia Beach, opposite Dillingham Field and back. Once in the water, Keola set a faster pace than I was used to, but the familiar call of "*Ae*" from Naomi in the stern and our responding "*Ho*" made me feel like I belonged.

The sea stayed calm on the trip out with only a small swell from the north. The outrigger skimmed easily over the smooth water. With the sun at our backs, it made for a pleasant paddle. Our return lap, facing into the sun with the trades starting up, was much more challenging. I was relieved to see the bridge at Hale'iwa come into view. I don't know whether it was the two-day layoff or just my trying to make a good impression, but I was tired. The thing about paddling is that you can stroke hard or soft while still maintaining the rhythm. I'd pulled hard and would probably be a little stiff by this evening.

We dragged the craft back up the beach and then circled once more for the *Mahalo* chant to give thanks to the land and sea. As I returned my paddle to the equipment box, Doc approached.

"Agapé, those of us who don't have to be at work right away usually meet back at the house for breakfast. Naomi and I would be pleased if you'd join us."

"Sounds good to me. I didn't have time for breakfast this morning."

"Great. If you want, you can leave your car here and ride up with us. I'll bring you back on my way to work."

"Okay, I'll just grab my stuff." I was pleased to be accepted into the group. *Good,* I thought*, it also means leaving the bugged rental car behind. Won't have to worry as much about being overheard.*

I slid into the rear seat of the SUV behind Doc and was pleased to see Terry take the other side. Barbara and Keola began walking across the bridge, Barbara pushing her bicycle. Doc started the car and turned onto Kam Highway.

"Terry," I began, "what do you do?"

"I work for the state government as an aide to Senator Fowler."

"You're quite a way from work, aren't you? The senator lives on the other side of the island, and the state offices are in Honolulu."

"Well, for the past year, one of my responsibilities has been overseeing the senator's yacht here in the harbor. Actually, it belongs to Naomi, but she's leasing it to him. He plans to use it to cover the islands during the upcoming campaign."

That must be the big craft I noticed yesterday.

Doc's place was back up Kam Highway, just before we got to Waimea. It was a good thing he was driving, as I would never have spotted the unmarked private street. The remote-controlled gate opened at our approach. The road continued through a thick tropical forest for a mile or so before opening onto a vast expanse of manicured lawn facing a massive two story Hawaiian-style home. A wide covered lanai completely surrounded the place.

Doc let us out at the portico leading to the front door, and Naomi ushered us in while Doc drove the car toward the large multi-car garage.

"This way," Naomi indicated when I paused in the expansive open-air living room. I noticed a large painting over the fireplace and several smaller pictures elsewhere in the room. They looked similar to the ones in my villa at Turtle Bay.

Terry was already heading for the interior courtyard. I could see a young man in a pale blue Hawaiian shirt and white pants standing near a buffet table before a natural lava rock fountain.

"Michael will prepare an omelet to your order," Naomi said, indicating the young man. "I'll have my usual please, Michael."

Terry was already filling a plate with fresh fruit at the nearby buffet, while our cook broke and whisked two eggs into a bowl. Then he added what looked like crumbled bacon, green onion, and sliced mushrooms, and poured the contents into a skillet set over the portable gas fire.

"That looks wonderful. I think I'll have the same, please," I requested.

"Would you like cheese on yours, also?" he asked. "I always add it at the last minute so it just melts and doesn't burn."

"Yes, cheese would be nice."

"I'll bring it to the table when it's ready," he said. "Please help yourself." He motioned toward the buffet on which was set an array of fresh fruits, breads, and other delights.

I collected a plate of fruit, mostly papaya, strawberries, and sliced bananas, but stayed away from the sweet rolls, bagels, and Hawaiian sweet bread. *Gerry would be pleased with my selection.*

I settled into a chair next to Terry and across from Naomi. Doc arrived, poured himself a glass of orange juice, and joined the table.

"So, Mr. Jones," he began. "What really brings you to our island?"

I've always found it's best to stay as close to the truth as possible and tell the same story each time. Makes remembering what you said easier. Too many lies can trip you up.

"Well, my outrigger team on Maui found Philip Fowler's body." From the corner of my eye, I saw Terry straighten slightly and take more notice of the conversation. "I'm retired from the NYPD and do some consulting work for Maui County. I was asked to see what I could find out about the case."

"Raul mentioned you were retired police," said Doc. "I thought you might be involved with this North Shore Development fiasco. Glad to hear you're not. It's been very contentious between the residents and the developers. The police arrest of some local protesters hasn't helped the situation."

"We've heard about it on the news," I replied, "but it probably isn't as bad as living in the middle of the conflict. How do you feel about it?"

Naomi responded first. "We're somewhat torn, to tell the truth. We love the natural beauty of the area and would hate to see wall-to-wall buildings. It would be nice to have the environment preserved. On the other hand, there was only open space here when Jerry, my first husband, and I built this house about ten years ago. We made sure the design blended into the surroundings and didn't stick out. We can't simply support banning all development since we built here ourselves and would love for others to share all this." She spread her arm to include the beautiful view out the back of the house.

Doc laughed. "You can't see the house until you're almost on top of it. Everyone is surprised the first time they come."

"You certainly did a nice job of making the most of your view while not taking away from the natural setting," I said.

"It was no accident," Naomi explained. "We were enamored of the designs of Charles William Dickey even before we arrived in the islands. Do you know who he was?"

"I don't think so."

"He was the architect credited with creating the Hawaiian plantation-style houses. Of course, he died about sixty years ago, but the legacy of his design remains. We hunted until we found a young architect who had studied the style. He was unknown when Jerry hired him, but he's gone on to some fame in his own right. This house has been featured in a couple of architectural magazines. I'll give you a tour before you leave."

"Thanks. I'd like that." From the center of the house where we sat, we could see the ocean. The rooms were all open with minimal furnishings. How I wished Gerry could be here with me. She'd have loved it.

While we were talking, Michael brought our food and coffee. I was enjoying this breakfast almost as much as sitting on the lanai at home.

"So what exactly are you doing here?" Terry asked. He hadn't forgotten my reason for being on the island.

"I'm trying to figure why a young man just starting out in life is dead. From all reports so far, he was well-liked and had no enemies."

"I'd have to agree," Terry said and the others nodded. "He was a good kid and a talented surfer. It's a real tragedy." He shook his head.

"The press is speculating that he might have been murdered. Do you know anything about it?" Naomi asked.

"I really can't say. The investigation is ongoing."

"Just losing a son is tragic enough. But murder..." She shuddered. "Keilani is a friend. She must be suffering. I've tried to call her, but her staff said she was indisposed. I'll try again later today."

Terry said nothing.

Chapter 10: Dead End

Doc dropped me off near my car after making me promise to join the team's next practice session on Wednesday, the day after tomorrow. I waved as the SUV carrying Doc and Terry headed across the bridge toward town. I wished I'd had more of a chance to talk to Terry, but he'd seemed reluctant to discuss anything after learning my purpose. Something about him sparked my detective's curiosity. It felt like he was hiding information, or at least not volunteering anything.

I slid into the front seat of the Cobalt, pulled my notebook from the glove compartment and spent a few moments transferring my thoughts and observations onto paper.

Check Terry's story – Neither the senator nor Bob mentioned having a yacht in Hale'iwa Harbor
Naomi Schwenck is a good friend of Keilani Fowler – She may have a way to meet her if direct approach doesn't work

I checked my watch. Nine o'clock. It had already been a busy but enjoyable morning. The paddle and breakfast were followed by a most pleasant tour of the house, during which I discovered that the paintings were, indeed, done by Doc.

"Painting has been his way of relaxing for years," Naomi said as we looked at another one, of a pool with palm trees in the background, hanging in a bedroom. "A friend who manages the hotel at Turtle Bay saw them and asked to buy some for the resort. That was several years ago. Since then, many of the rooms, cottages, and villas feature Doc's work. Of course, he doesn't charge nearly enough for them. But he gets a kick out of seeing his effort appreciated by others."

"There are two in my villa, and I must admit I enjoy looking at them."

She smiled. "That's his greatest reward. Since neither of us has children, we're not worried about leaving a fortune to heirs."

"I guess that explains why Doc's not concerned about how much he gets for his art."

She gave me a warm smile. "His work for charity over the years has meant so much to him. We've both arranged that whatever money we leave will go to continue the work he's begun. And that feels right."

Spending the short time I had with Naomi and Doc gave me a greater appreciation for both of them as well as an understanding of what Tommy had said about them. They were good together.

I still had almost an entire day left. But I wasn't here on vacation.

"Better get back to work, Mr. Detective," I said aloud. "What next?"

Well, there are several choices. I can talk to Tommy and Toshi again to see if they've come up with anything new or call Watanabe or... Hmmm, I still need to question the other family members. The Senator said Mr. Hillman would be available. Time to call in a marker.

I dialed the number Bob had given me.

"Senator Fowler's office, Hillman speaking."

"Bob, Agapé Jones. Can you arrange for me to talk with Mrs. Fowler and Slade sometime today?"

"I'll see what I can do. Slade left early this morning, probably headed for the North Shore. Mrs. Fowler is at home but not seeing anyone. I don't recommend your driving out here today as the press and paparazzi are still mobbing the front gate."

"Do you know exactly where Slade was going?" I pulled out my notebook and pencil.

"Not really. He doesn't tell anyone his plans."

"Well, see if you can arrange for a meeting with Mrs. Fowler tomorrow. Perhaps somewhere away from the estate."

"I'll let you know," he said and hung up.

I had the distinct feeling I was being stonewalled. Not from anything Bob said. He appeared to be very cooperative. It was just a nagging suspicion. And I didn't expect a return call.

Maybe I'll have better luck at Typhoon Tommy's. Besides, per-

haps I can find out about getting a surfboard for Malcolm in time for Christmas.

I started the car and headed onto Kam Highway and across the bridge into Hale'iwa.

Entering the shop, I saw Toshi behind the counter.

"Hi, I'm looking for Tommy. Is he here?"

"Sorry. He's on his boat fishing. Said he needed a day off. Does that sometime. Maybe I can help."

I wasn't sure how much information Tommy had given to Toshi, so I decided I'd start with Mal's board.

"I told Tommy I was thinking of getting a surfboard for my grandson for Christmas. He suggested I talk to the guys from Liquid Excitement."

"You in luck," he said as he glanced toward the door as the bell over the door sounded. "Hi, Jake," he greeted the newcomer. I recognized him from the pictures Tommy had shown me. He looked a little older and more lined than I remembered.

"Yo, Tosh," Jake replied as he approached. "Got a check for me?"

"Yeah. Oh, and this guy wants a board."

"Agapé Jones," I said, shaking his hand.

"I'm sure we can do something for you," he replied, sizing me up.

I laughed. "It's not for me," I said. "I wanted to get an extra special one for my fifteen-year-old grandson."

"There may be one here in the shop that would work."

"Well..." I hesitated. "I thought it would be cool if I

could tell him I saw his board made right from the beginning. He just moved to California and has talked about learning to surf. I'd like to know a few details about something that interests the kid. I don't get to be an authority on much anymore."

Jake laughed. "I know about that. I have a twelve-year-old myself. Dad and all adults have become pretty stupid lately. I keep hoping he'll outgrow it."

"He will, but it won't be for a few years," I answered. "All teenage boys go through the surly stage. You know, when they develop the Elvis sneer. I think my son was about thirty and a father himself before I knew anything again. Now he actually asks my advice."

Toshi opened the register and handed Jake an envelope.

"Thanks, Tosh. And tell that no-good brother of yours that he's supposed to be running a business here. I saw his whaler chugging out of the harbor this morning. How's he supposed to sell our boards if he's not here?"

"Oh, and I guess Wacko, Cho, and Jamie don't ever close up once in a while. And you don't ever go surfing during the day. Huh?"

"Hey, man, that's my livelihood," Jake said with a laugh. "I get paid to do that."

"Sure." Toshi shook his head.

Jake turned to me. "Come on. Let me take you to the shop and we'll see what we can do for ya."

We both waved to Toshi as we left. Turning the corner, I followed Jake toward the converted warehouse.

"Damn. The cars aren't here. That probably means the guys are out joyriding in Jamie's souped-up, thirty-three-foot Grady."

He tried the door, but the place was locked.

"I'll have to give you a rain check. I didn't think I'd need my key. I was on a photo shoot this morning and haven't been in. Doesn't look like the guys have been here either." He sounded annoyed. "Jamie's got more money than sense."

"Tommy told me a little about him."

"Sometimes I feel so sorry for the kid when I realize he can't ever stand on a surfboard again and feel the power of the waves. Then I think about everything he's wasting, and I just get mad. His parents give him all the latest toys, and he's like a spoiled brat. Doesn't take care of anything."

"How so?" I wasn't sure where this was going, but he seemed to need to vent.

"He has three custom wheelchairs. A couple for racing. One is powered and is customized for his boat. It's even low enough so he can get around to sand the boards. He has the job to help him feel useful. But his folks seem to be doing everything they can to enable him to remain a cripple."

"Sounds like you really care about him."

"Of course I do. But I just don't know what to do about it. And hanging out with Wacko isn't in his best interest, either. That guy fried a few too many brain cells years ago. For all I know, he's still using."

"What about Jamie?"

"Don't think so. He's on some pretty powerful meds. I

hope he wouldn't screw that up. But..."

"Well, thanks for offering to help," I said.

"Come back again when you see cars parked. That way you'll know one of us is here. Meanwhile, why don't you leave your grandson's vitals with Toshi, I mean, things like height and weight and where he lives. That way, I'll know what kind of board to design. Oh, and write down a number where I can reach you."

"I'll do that," I answered. "By the way, have you seen Slade Fowler around here today?"

He looked at me a little strangely. "Why you looking for him?"

"I heard about his brother and wanted to extend my condolences. I called the house, but he wasn't home."

"Did his family tell you he'd be here?"

"Well..."

Jake shook his head. "Haven't seen him in a while. His dad was one of the initial investors in the business. I guess he hoped Slade would take an interest. But he didn't. I've seen him around Honolulu, though. Drives a nice car and always seems to have lots of money to throw around."

"I guess his folks are generous..." I hoped he'd give me more information.

"I don't think so. I overheard him talking to his dad on the phone. He was pretty angry when he hung up. Seems his father cut him off."

"How long ago was that?"

He thought for a minute. "A couple of weeks. Maybe a little more."

"Before his brother died, then?"

"Oh, yeah. Must have been at least a week or so earlier. Haven't seen him since."

I wanted to ask Jake to let me know if he saw Slade, but I couldn't think of a good enough reason on the spot, and I didn't want everyone knowing why I was really there.

"If you see him, let him know I asked about him."

"Will do. But I doubt that'll be any time soon."

We parted. I left the information with Toshi. I made a few notes, then drove back up to the hotel where I showered and dressed. It felt good to finally get the salt and sand off.

The blinking light on the phone indicated there was a message. The desk clerk said that a Mr. Watanabe would like me to call him back at my earliest convenience.

Since the room was bugged, I grabbed my cell and walked down to the beach until I found an open spot where no one could listen in.

"Agapé Jones here."

"Mr. Jones, I thought you would be interested in the toxicology results on our friend." He seemed overly cautious and I wondered if he might be concerned about being overheard.

"Yes. I'd be very interested," I responded.

"The findings were negative."

"No drugs?" I asked.

"No. They are certain."

That seems to rule Nicki out. And she was my only real suspect with motive and opportunity. Where do I go from here?

"Thank you for telling me," I said. "Anything else I should know?"

"Not a thing. What have you found out there?"

"Nothing important. At least, not yet."

"Ah…" I could almost see him nodding.

"Please keep me fully informed," I said.

"And you'll let me know if you uncover anything," he responded. It was a statement, not a request.

"Will do."

We hung up and I wondered if he knew how much of a poker game we were playing. I was already aware that he knew more than he was disclosing. *Why would he keep me in the dark?*

Unfortunately, I'd told the truth. I hadn't a clue except for the one Duke had given me. And until those tests came back, I wouldn't be able to follow up on that.

It wasn't that I didn't trust Watanabe, but I felt I needed confirmation. I called Duke.

"Agapé, what's up?" he asked when I identified myself.

"Watanabe just called with the tox results."

"So you know they didn't find anything in his system."

"Yes."

"Looks like his squeaky-clean image wasn't an illusion."

"That's what I've heard from everyone I've talked to. He was a good kid, smart and talented, and everyone liked him."

"Doesn't give you much to work on, does it?"

"Nope. No one seems to have a motive. I thought his girlfriend might be a possibility since she had access to drugs.

But the results just took care of that one." I was secretly relieved. I like Nicki. And I'm rarely wrong when it comes to my sense of people.

"Well, keep at it. I don't think he put that hole in his chest by himself. And I don't think he paddled all the way from Oahu to Maui. Something doesn't add up."

"Yeah. But all I have at the moment are zeroes."

"By the way, we still don't have a positive ID on the junk in his ears and nose, but we're releasing the body in about an hour. I guess the rumors about a family feud are real. But his parents have the final say. He'll be transported back to Oahu later today."

We said goodbye, and since it was almost noon, I decided to get a light lunch. It was hard to imagine that I could be hungry after that breakfast, but maybe a little nourishment would provide enlightenment.

Chapter 11: An Unexpected Invitation

I went back into Hale'iwa intending to drive through a fast food place. I passed Matsumoto's and decided to stop there instead. It's a legend on the North Shore and claims to serve the best shave ice in the islands. (There are several other places that would challenge the title, but locals swear there's no comparison.) A line snaked around the corner on the outside, and the dirt lot next door was crowded. But I managed to find enough room to park.

While I waited to order, I had to decide exactly what I wanted. There were twenty-four choices listed on the sign. In addition to the expected flavors, there were some uniquely Hawaiian ones like *lilikoi* (passion fruit), mango, *lihing mui* (dried plum), *lychee* (sweet Chinese fruit), and coconut. Everything sounded good, so I was glad they offered combinations. That always appeals to me. I could add ice cream, too. They make their own, so it would be healthier, right? I wasn't sure about the adzuki beans. The guys on Maui tell me they're good, but they'd just add calories, and Gerry might not like that. She probably wouldn't like the ice cream either, but I'd only tell her if she asked.

I entered. Inside it looked like an ancient general store with dusty shelves and boxes piled to the ceiling. They also sold T-shirts to the tourists, but the big draw was the shave ice. Finally it was my turn.

"I'll have a watermelon, *lilikoi*, and coconut with ice cream." It was a tough but mouthwatering decision.

I took my sweet, cool lunch and drove to Hale'iwa Ali'i Beach Park, sipping on the way. I grabbed my towel and notebook, walked to the same hill where I'd sat the day before and found a shady spot. After spreading the towel on the ground, I leaned back against a palm and enjoyed the rest of my treat along with the view.

The big yacht was still in the harbor, but there was no sign of Terry. In fact, it appeared no one was on board. A few boats moved inside the breakwater, but for some reason, the beach was deserted. I figured all the tourists were up at the better-known spots and the locals could see the surf had died down. I wished it had been this small in the early hours when we were fighting it while paddling.

The gusty early-morning breeze had settled into the gentle trades I loved. The feel of the cooler air relieved the warmth of the sun.

Since moving here, I've become religious about sun block. Some people think that dark-skinned folks like me don't need it. But I got a bad burn when we first arrived, and Gerry keeps reminding me that I could also get skin cancer.

So I make sure to use it. Paddling reinforced the need.

When all the shave ice and ice cream were gone, I started to make more notes.

Slade's dad cut off his funds – Motive?
Where is Slade?
Both Tommy and Jamie have fishing boats – kept in Hale'iwa Harbor?
No drugs found in the body
Slake said Wacko had done drugs and might still be doing them
Why isn't Watanabe telling me everything?

What else? Nothing. That's what.

"Oh Lovey, how I wish you were here to talk to," I whispered.

In my detective days, I'd often stop by my mother's place on the way home. It wasn't only for her great pecan pie and hot coffee. She would listen to me complain about how a particular case I was working was going or, more often, not going. She was my cheering section, sounding board, and, on occasion, she scolded as well. Everyone called her Lovey. I wasn't sure what her given name was until I saw her death certificate. Gertrude didn't suit her, but Lovey did. And I miss her. Especially in the middle of a tough case. Sometimes I had too many suspects. This time I had none.

Lovey, where do I go from here?

'Baby, you start at the beginning.' I could almost hear her voice.

But where's the beginning?

I closed my eyes and clearly heard her laughter. I loved her laugh. It came from somewhere deep inside her and burst forth with no restraint. '*Where did your young man start out? Who saw him last? What did he say? Those are the basics, son. Once you know those, you'll know how he came to you.'*

What do you mean, came to me?

'Well, darlin', God entrusted him into your care. You didn't go lookin' for him. He came to you. And he's your responsibility. You owe it to him and his people to find out what happened.'

Gee, thanks for adding that responsibility.

She didn't laugh this time. '*Things happen for a reason, son. You know I always believed that. It's no accident you're where you are. You are needed. And you can do it. I know it and so does God, or you wouldn't be involved.'*

But I still don't know where to start.

'Don't play stupid with me. You ask. It's what you do best. You ask that girlfriend. You ask his family. You keep asking until you get the answers.' Then her voice softened. *'I know you can do it. You're the best. I raised you that way. And, son, I'm so very proud of you.'*

She was right. Back to the beginning. Where was Philip before he died? Who saw him last? What was his mood? And finally, how the heck did he get to Maui?

I was exhausted. I knew Nicki wouldn't be home from work for several hours, and she was my best lead. It was obvious that Bob wasn't going to be too helpful. Watanabe was less than forthcoming.

I lay down on the towel to rest and think.

The next thing I knew, my watch told me the afternoon was waning. I was feeling a little hungry but not enough for a large hotel dinner. The shave ice had worn off. But another 'world's greatest hamburger' or *pupus* by the pool didn't appeal either. Maybe something in town would interest me.

Passing through Hale'iwa, I spotted Foodland and thought, *I could pick up fruit and sandwich fixings along with some drinks to take back to the hotel.*

I entered the store, shunned the shopping cart, and picked up a plastic basket. I've noticed if I push a cart through a store, I feel obligated to fill it. The basket was a better solution.

In the deli, I found a prepackaged egg salad sandwich that looked good. I added a couple of bananas, a papaya, a bag of chips, the healthier baked ones for snacking, and a six-pack of diet soda. I also remembered a disposable camera so I could take pictures of my room to show Gerry.

At checkout, I placed my items on the conveyor.

"Mr. Jones," said a voice. "You're still here. You must like our little town."

I glanced up and recognized the person ahead in line as Nicki's next-door neighbor. When we spoke at Nicki's house, I hadn't given her my name.

"Nice to see you," I stammered. "Sorry, what was your name again?"

"It's Malia," she responded. "Nicki told me all about you and why you're here. Now, you be kind to that girl. She's been through a lot lately and doesn't need any more trouble." She waggled her finger at me and her voice sounded like a grandmother scolding a small child for misbehaving. I almost laughed.

"I'll be kind, you can be sure of that," I said.

The checker was loading two large cloth bags. I noticed one held a whole chicken from the store's ready-to-serve heated cabinet.

She hefted her bags and said, "Till we meet again, then," and left.

I paid for my items, exited the store, and noticed her walking. I got in my car and caught up to her.

"Would you like a lift?" I inquired. "After all, you can trust me. I'm not one of those pesky reporters you accused me of being when we first met."

"I guess it's all right. Nicki says you're retired police. Besides, my feet are killing me."

I leaned over and opened the door. She placed her bags in the backseat and got in on the passenger side.

"*Mahalo*," she said. "I've lived here all my life and walked from town thousands of times. But lately I'm slowing down, and the path seems to be getting longer."

"All your life?" I repeated. I knew this conversation was being monitored or recorded, but it was probably okay. I didn't expect any critical revelations from a neighbor.

"Do you know how they named my town?"

"No, I don't, but you'll probably tell me," I said as I pulled the car onto the road toward her home. I smiled. I could sense another Hawaiian 'talk story' beginning.

"*Hale'iwa* means 'house of the frigate bird' or *'iwa.'* When I was a little girl, there was a beautiful hotel with that name right across from the harbor. People visiting my family would stay there. The former manager, old Mr. I'aukea who had once served as royal chamberlain to the Kalākauas at 'Iolani Palace, was a family friend. He said the place was named after the female seminary that missionaries built on that site in the 1830s. The Hale'iwa Hotel was torn down after the Second World War, but by then the town and beach had acquired the name."

"Very interesting," I commented, but I knew she wasn't done.

"In all my years, I have yet to see an *'iwa'* or, as you mainlanders call it, the 'frigate bird' land here. I think they need a high place or a cliff to take off from, and there's none nearby. The ancients called them storm birds as they often flew inland just before a storm approached."

I paused to let oncoming traffic pass before making the left from Kam Highway to Hale'iwa Road. Scanning the rearview mirror, I noticed the same black sedan with darkened windows following us through the turn.

Better have the police run the license, I thought as I noted the plate number. *I'll add it to my notebook as soon as I can.*

Malia was still talking, but I had missed part of the conversation.

"...Then, when Mano and I were married, we settled first in a house in Mokulē'ia Beach before moving back here. I'm grateful for the ride as the chicken will be much warmer for dinner."

"Glad I could help," I interrupted. "Say, do any of your neighbors drive a black Nissan Sentra?"

"No, no one I know. All those foreign cars look alike to me anyway. I never learned to drive. Mano used to, but he broke his hip last year and doesn't leave the house much anymore."

I wanted to ask her just what Nicki had told her about me but needed to wait until we were away from the rental car and its electronic eavesdropper.

I pulled to a stop in front of her house. The black sedan was parked where I'd seen it before. No one got out.

"I'll walk you to the door," I offered.

"That won't be necessary, Mr. Jones. You've done so much already. I'm sure Mano will appreciate hot chicken for a change. Usually it's just warm by the time I walk home."

"No problem," I said as I got out and rounded the car to open her door. Actually, my stiffened leg was still feeling the effects of the morning's paddle. But I wanted to ask some more questions.

I took one bag, she carried the other, and we proceeded to the front door. As we climbed the three steps to the porch, I could see a very dirty and partially rusted-out Ford wagon parked beside the house. The bumper sticker read "*No Mall at Sharks Cove*." At the front door, multiple pairs of sandals lay side-by-side, as if awaiting the return of their owners. Malia handed me her bag while she fished out her key.

"For years we never locked the door. But it's not as safe now," she explained as she turned the key.

I carried both bags and followed her into the tiny kitchen.

The house was small and immaculately kept but crowded with knickknacks, pictures, books—a lifetime of memories. Shelves to hold the items covered nearly every wall of each room I entered. Over the kitchen stove hung an assortment of pans, lids, and other utensils. I placed the bags on the table.

An elderly Hawaiian man with thinning white hair entered the room. He was dressed in a neatly-pressed Hawaiian shirt and white pleated pants. Even without shoes he appeared quite regal, holding himself erect, although he walked with a slight shuffle as if unsure of his balance.

"This is my husband, Mano," Malia said. "Mano, this is Agapé Jones."

"Mr. Jones." The man took my hand in a firm grip, belying his frail appearance. "Nicki has told us much about you. It's so nice to finally meet. Please sit."

"I really should be getting on," I said.

"Nonsense, you're staying for dinner, of course," Malia insisted as she unloaded her groceries. "I won't take no for an answer. We have plenty. I'll just throw together a salad and we'll be ready. Mano, set another place at the table, please."

I had to admit, a warm meal with a friendly couple as opposed to eating a cold sandwich alone in the hotel was appealing. "Okay, you've convinced me, but only if you'll call me

Agapé. Can I help with anything?"

"Not a thing," she answered as she bustled around the kitchen.

Soon the simple meal was on the table, and we took our seats. The smell of the sliced chicken reminded me that I was hungry. I wished I'd been able to bring a bottle of wine or dessert or something. But their hospitality was warm and genuine. I felt honored.

"I wish it were real *huli huli* chicken, grilled over an open fire with Mano's special barbeque sauce," she apologized.

Mano smiled.

"This is just perfect. I don't think my wife would approve of the sauce."

Malia nodded. "We're watching what we eat these days, too."

"Tell me about the sticker on the back of your car," I said, turning to Mano.

He seemed a little surprised but anxious to tell someone. It was as though he welcomed an audience.

"They wanted to build a huge shopping mall with fifty-three stores and an underground garage for two-hundred cars across the street from Shark's Cove. We don't have streets or power or anything else to support something that big. I was involved with Surfrider Foundation's protest of the project. Toward the end, it got pretty radical. But we finally defeated the developers."

"Congratulations. I've heard there are still protests regarding local development here."

He looked very intense as he answered. "You need to understand. We're not opposed to all change here on the North Shore. Change is inevitable. We love seeing people enjoy the views and the natural beauty and playing on our beaches. We just don't want enormous developments which spoil the landscape, overburden our resources, and destroy our historic sites. The locals want to keep the country feel of the area. That's what attracts tourists. We don't want to become another Kaanapali with wall-to-wall people and noise."

"Could you tell me about the current situation?" I asked.

"If you're really interested." His face grew even more serious.

This could take a while.

Chapter 12: The Developers

Mano sat back in his chair and took a deep breath. "Several developers plan to build five new hotels and one thousand resort condominiums at Kawela Bay and Turtle Bay. I belong to a group called the 'Defend Oahu Coalition.' We protest from time to time, trying to save the North Shore. Our goal is to preserve our surfing reefs and beaches. This community prides itself on being rural, small town, friendly, and uncongested. It's like maintaining a little bit of old Hawaii in the modern world."

Malia nodded in agreement.

"But you said change was inevitable," I replied.

"And it is. What we're protesting is the never-ending onslaught of developers who want to take advantage of the location and destroy the character of the area. Another group I belonged to, the 'Save Sunset Beach Coalition,' succeeded in blocking a plan to develop dozens of condo units along the Pupukea/Paumalu Plateau overlooking most of the surfing beaches. We worked with the federal government and the state of Hawaii to buy the property and preserve it forever as a park."

"That must have given you satisfaction," I observed.

"It did," he answered. "But we can't afford to let up. We aren't about to kiss our country lifestyle goodbye without a fight. Unfortunately, some of the younger protesters are threatening violence. Several have been arrested, and the situation is escalating. I don't agree with that at all. Peaceful protest is required, not physical threats."

"Do you really think it could become dangerous?"

Mano looked thoughtful for a moment. "It already is. The developers have a lot of money invested. Rumor has it that key government officials may have been bought off. Everyone from outside is considered suspect. That includes you, Mr. Jones. So please be careful."

"It's really that serious?"

Both Mano and Malia nodded together.

"Mano, have you noticed the black car with the tinted windows parked at the end of your street?"

He looked uncomfortable. "Yes. It's been there off and on for the past week."

"Do you know anything about the driver or what it's doing here?"

Mano shook his head. "I've never seen anyone get out. But it makes me nervous."

I didn't tell him about the car following us to his house. He'd have been even more disturbed, so I decided to change the subject.

"Do you know anything about surfboards?" I asked. "I'm thinking of getting one for my grandson."

His face lit up. "Oh, yes. I've been surfing since before you were born."

"But not any more," Malia was quick to add as she gave him a stern look.

I recognized the same tone Gerry sometimes uses, and I didn't want to end up in the middle. "What should I consider when ordering a board for him?" I figured this was a safe topic.

Mano described how the person's height and weight and type of surf they'd be in all contributed to the length and shape of the board. It was actually very interesting.

While we were discussing the finer points of surfboard design, Malia left the room and returned with a faded photo of a teenaged Mano next to Duke Kahanamoku, each of them posed with their surfboards towering behind them, both grinning at the camera.

When he saw the picture, Mano laughed. "Oh, to be that young and fit again!"

"He was quite a catch," Malia said and smiled at him.

The rest of the evening was spent with my hosts telling stories of old Hawaii. I found myself laughing and truly enjoying the time I shared with them.

I was amazed when I glanced at my watch and discovered it was nearly ten o'clock. I'd been up early and wasn't really tired. But I would be soon.

"Thank you again for a wonderful evening," I said as Malia led me through their darkened living room. She turned on the porch light.

"It was our pleasure, Mr. Jones."

"Agapé," I reminded her.

She laughed. "We grew up in a more formal time, I'm afraid. And our families insisted that we use only proper forms of address." She shook her head. "The young people to-day think we grew up with the dinosaurs."

I laughed with her. "I know just what you mean."

She grew serious. "Take care."

"I will," I assured her and walked to my car. The black sedan was still parked down the street. All the lights were out.

I drove carefully back to the hotel. No one followed me.

I retrieved the grocery bag and headed to my room. The sandwich had spent too much time in the car, but it was a small sacrifice in exchange for the good company and simple meal I'd had.

The first thing I did was to write down the license number of the black car with this note:

Ask Duke to run the plate

I wished I could have asked Watanabe, but I wasn't sure if he was being completely truthful with me. And I had no one else. Besides, I trusted Duke.

I started to make more notes when I noticed the red light on the phone. The desk said Gerry had called about nine-thirty. All of a sudden, I missed her. Even though it was late, I dialed our number.

"Hello," she answered.

Funny, she doesn't sound as though I woke her.

"Hi, babe," I said, trying to sound cheerful.

"Hi, yourself," she replied. The laughter in her voice told me she wasn't mad. "Where have you been? I was starting to worry."

"I was invited for dinner by a lovely Hawaiian woman."

"Oh, really?"

"Uh, yes. And her husband. They're both about eighty."

"That's a likely story."

"I gave her a lift home from the store, and she insisted I stay."

"So, you're picking up total strangers from the store, now?" She wasn't buying my abbreviated version of the story.

"Actually, I met her yesterday. She's the neighbor of the young man's girlfriend." It was then I realized that I hadn't asked the old folks anything about what Nicki had said to them. But apparently it all must have been good, whatever it was, since they had invited me into their home.

"Well, I'm glad you weren't alone and that you had a good time. How are things going?"

"Slowly," I admitted. "I need to put together an action plan and then get going on it. But I did get some information on a surfboard I want to get for Mal." I figured changing the subject might distract her.

"And just how much is this little gift going to cost?"

"Well, I don't have all the information yet. But I might get to help them make it."

"You sound just like you did when you described the swing set you were going to build for the kids."

"I must admit, I'm starting to get excited about the idea."

Gerry sighed. "I guess it doesn't matter what it's going to cost. Once you get this involved, there's no turning back." Then she laughed. "Have fun."

"I will. But I miss you. I wish you were here."

"So do I. But I hope you can get your part of this...whatever it is...wrapped up soon."

I remembered my cover story. "They're still running in different directions and need someone to keep them focused." It sounded good to me.

"Well, hurry up and straighten them out."

"I'll try, honey. I love you."

"Love you, too. Good night."

"Sweet dreams."

I sat with the sound of the dial tone buzzing in my ear for a moment. The room seemed even emptier, and I vowed I'd get up early and take those pictures. I wanted her to share the experience. And I wanted her to know I missed her.

I wasn't sure I liked someone eavesdropping on my personal conversations with my wife, but I didn't say anything I was worried about them hearing.

I returned to my notebook and made a list of the people and places to approach in the morning. It would be a busy day.

Chapter 13: A Better Day in Paradise

The soft ukulele of Iz's version of "Over the Rainbow" gently brought me awake at six-thirty.

Much better than that tacky alarm buzzer, I thought. *Good thing I found a local station and changed the clock to the radio setting last night.*

I waited until the entire song was over before turning off the alarm. Israel Kamakawiwo'ole may be gone, but his music will live on, especially here in the islands.

I expect this to be a better day. Thanks to Lovey, I finally have a plan.

Following my morning PT, I poured water in the hotel-provided two-cup coffeemaker and dropped in the pre-measured packet of Kona blend, the real stuff, not the decaf. While it brewed, I showered, shaved, and dressed.

When I pulled back the drapes, morning light filled the room. It was still too early for phone calls, so I opened the refrigerator, retrieved the papaya I'd purchased the day before, sliced it and removed the seeds, then put it on a plate along with a sliced banana. I took my fruit and coffee to the table on the outdoor lanai. As I ate, I savored the morning breeze and the fragrance of the islands. The only thing missing to make the scene complete was Gerry sitting opposite me.

After clearing the remnants of my breakfast, picking up my dirty clothes, and smoothing the bedspread, I grabbed the disposable camera and took some pictures of the room and the view for Gerry, still wishing she could be there to enjoy it with me.

With my second cup of coffee, cell phone, and notebook in hand, I contemplated returning to the lanai. *Better get a little more distance from the room. There could be a listening device out there, too.*

I turned down the path toward the point and the main building of the hotel. The outdoor pool was situated above a low rock-strewn cliff. Small waves rounded Kuilima Point, swept past the pool area, and on into Turtle Bay. This location gave me a unique side view of passing waves, kind of like watching a parade. Two kids on boogie boards were catching small rollers near the cliff. A couple of surfers were waiting for the bigger ones farther out. The area was deserted except for the riders and one of the hotel staff on pool-cleaning duty. I settled into a chair on the far side of the deck and flipped open my notebook.

Ask Duke to run the plate

I hit the speed dial for Duke's cell phone and connected.

It didn't take long before I heard, "Agapé, what can I do for you? Have you made any progress?"

"Not much. I've pretty well eliminated my only suspect, but there's something you can do for me."

"Sure, if I can."

"I'd like you to run the plate on a suspicious black Nissan. It's been parked on Nicki's street, always in a different place, and no one ever gets out." I didn't mention that it had followed me.

"Sure."

I gave him the rest of the description and the number.

"Okay, I'll get my guys on it. Anything else?"

"Not right now, maybe later."

"Okay. I'm here if you need me."

"Thanks." It was reassuring to know I had Duke on my side. He was reliable and honest, two qualities I depend on in other cops.

It was eight-thirty, and Bob should be at work. So I could get to the next item on my list:

Call Bob for meetings with family

He picked up on the first ring. "Senator Fowler's office. Bob Hillman speaking."

"Agapé Jones. Have you been able to arrange a meeting with Mrs. Fowler or Slade?"

I wasn't surprised at his answer. "No. I'm sorry. The press is still swarming the house, and the preparations for the funeral have everyone occupied. Perhaps at the end of the week..."

"Well, do your best and let me know if something can be arranged sooner."

"Will do." Click.

I hadn't expected any help from that quarter, but I wanted to be sure I'd given him an opportunity before exercising other options.

Call Doc and Naomi

I punched the number. Naomi answered.

"Good morning. I hope I didn't disturb you," I began.

"Good heavens, no. When we're paddling, we're up before dawn, and we keep to the same schedule on our off days. Doc went to the hospital early. You'd hardly know he's supposed to be retired." She chuckled.

"I seem to be so busy now that I'm retired, I don't know when I had time to work," I replied.

"I'm glad you called," she said.

"Why's that?"

"I wanted to notify everyone about the big paddle-out for Philip Fowler tomorrow. The club's been asked to take part."

"I'd be honored. I've never seen a paddle-out before."

She chuckled. "Even if you had, it probably wouldn't be as grand as this one. He was not only a famous local surfer, but a member of an *ali'i* family. That's Hawaiian royalty. It's going to be like a state funeral, Hawaiian style."

"Where do we fit in?"

"The events will start at nine o'clock. There'll be a service at *Kawaiaha'o,* the Great Stone Church in Honolulu. During the days of the monarchy, it was called 'The Church of the *Ali'i.*' Today, it's sometimes referred to as 'The State Church of Hawaii.' I'm sure you've heard of it."

Duke had told me about the church and the paddle-out, but at the time I hadn't expected to be taking part. "Yes, that's the one where the choir sings in Hawaiian, isn't it?"

"Right. Then the family and all their friends will drive to Hale'iwa where the last part of the ceremony will begin."

"Are you going to the church service?" I asked.

"No. Since Keilani asked me to participate with the club, I can't make the service."

I'd hoped we might be able to get there and still make it back in time. I'd missed church on Sunday by flying here, and I still wanted to hear that choir in person. I made a mental note to plan a weekend when I could come back with Gerry.

"When and where will you need me?" I asked.

"We'll meet on the beach about eleven to get ready. We want to allow enough time to find each other and get the canoe in position."

I heard papers rustling.

Then she continued, "Let's see… I'll bring leis for everyone. Then we'll wait for the double-hulled voyaging canoe to emerge from the harbor at about noon. It will carry the family, the local *kahuna,* and the ashes. As soon as the canoe appears, we'll take to the water to escort it offshore beyond the surf line, along with a large number of surfers on their boards."

"Sounds impressive."

"It will be. We'll form a circle about a mile from shore. Then the *kahuna* will chant and spread the ashes. It's very beautiful."

"What happens then?"

"We'll meet back on the beach for a huge luau where people will 'talk story' for the rest of the afternoon. This could last long into the evening."

"I'll be there. Count on it."

"Thanks. We appreciate your filling in. But I didn't give you a chance to tell me why you called."

"I was curious. Have you talked to Mrs. Fowler?"

"Yes. As a matter of fact, she called this morning to make sure we'd be there tomorrow. I was just about to phone you when I picked up, and there you were."

"I've been trying to make an appointment to speak with her, but she's never available."

"Keilani's been keeping to herself and avoiding reporters."

"How would you suggest I approach her?"

"Well, I know where she'll be around eleven today."

"And where's that?"

"She gets her hair done at a little shop called Nani Hulu in Kailua, owned by an old school friend of hers. Keilani recommended it to me when we first met. She has an appointment today."

"Do you think she might be willing to give me a few minutes?"

"She knows you're helping the police on the case, and she wants to talk with you."

Naomi gave me the address of the shop and driving directions.

Finally, a break.

"Thanks for the information. I'll see you on the beach at dawn."

"We've decided to skip practice since we'll be paddling later on."

"Okay. I'll see you around eleven, then."

"*Aloha*."

"*Aloha,* and *mahalo* for your help."

It was about the same distance to get to Kailua whether I returned to Waipahu and then across the Pali Highway or went east along the coast. The coast road was probably a little shorter, but I felt better taking the main highway. Whichever direction I chose, I needed to get going right away.

Chapter 14: Meeting Keilani

As I drove across the island, I kept checking to see if I was being tailed. I wasn't.

I'd have liked to enjoy the lush greenery of the rain forest along the way, but 'liquid sunshine' made the road a little slick. At last I crested the hill and saw Kaneohe Bay in the distance. Pali Highway is pretty winding and took all my concentration, what with tourist traffic and the wet conditions.

The rain had stopped by the time I arrived in Kailua. I followed Naomi's directions and was surprised to find Nani Hulu in a small strip mall. I pulled the Cobalt into a shaded parking spot near the salon entrance. Still no sign of a tail.

I was about fifteen minutes early and hoped I had gotten there ahead of Mrs. Fowler.

I had expected the stretch limo, so was surprised to see a silver Mercedes pull up in front. Clarence emerged from the driver's side, walked around, and opened the rear passenger door.

Mrs. Fowler was smaller than I'd expected. While she

entered, Clarence guarded the door, surveying the parking lot in what I identified as a professional manner. I'd suspected he acted as bodyguard for the family. His actions seemed to confirm this.

Still on full alert, Clarence returned to the car and parked next to me. Seeming to ignore my presence, he got out, locked up, strolled back, and leaned against the wall next to the salon entrance. He put a cigarette to his lips, then looked straight at me. A slight head gesture indicated I should join him.

As I approached, he pointed to his right. I stepped beside him. He turned so his body shielded me from street view.

"Got a match?" he asked.

"Sorry, I don't smoke," I replied. "Isn't there a lighter in the Mercedes?"

"Too many ears in the car. Besides, Miz Fowler don't like me smokin' inside. Bad habit anyway." He returned the cigarette to the pack in his shirt pocket.

I nodded in agreement.

"You here to talk to her?" he asked.

"Yes. I've been trying ever since the day you drove me to the house. Any chance today?"

"Might be." He hadn't committed, but I sensed a possible opening.

"Where's the limo?" I asked.

Clarence chuckled. "The gardener's takin' it for a nice spin up to Pearl City. Got a whole lot of press taggin' along behind. I took the senator to work as usual without bein' followed. Those reporters don't want to see him. They want to get to his wife and son."

"Nice evasion," I said.

"Thought so myself." He grinned.

It was getting hot standing in the sun.

"I'm a little thirsty. How about you?" I asked.

"They have smoothies and soft drinks next door," he volunteered. "That's where I usually hang out while waitin' for her to finish."

He led the way.

On one side of the little store was a sandwich shop where the menu indicated lots of healthy choices. I noticed most of them included sprouts and whole grain breads.

The other side was where I was instinctively drawn. I felt a little déjà vu, since many of the smoothie flavors painted on the wall were similar to the choices I'd had the day before at Matsumoto's. In addition, you could add wheat grass, brewer's yeast, protein powder, yogurt, sherbet, or ice cream. I love choices and settled on raspberry, mango, and peach with raspberry sherbet, staying clear of the twigs and grass. They somehow don't belong in a drink.

Clarence went for a large chocolate with ice cream. It looked good, but I knew Gerry would have a fit. The sherbet was bad enough, but after all, there was fresh fruit with it.

We picked a table at the window where we could both see the parking lot. Anyone approaching the salon next door would be in view.

We enjoyed our cold drinks while keeping watch.

"Where's Slade today?" I asked.

"Don't know. I don't drive him any more since he got that fancy sports car. Thought I spotted his Lamborghini on my trip here. Hard to miss since it's the only one on the island painted red with black racing stripes."

"Do you know where he might have been going?"

"No clue. The boy's been real distant ever since his daddy cut off his money."

"When was that?"

He paused to take a sip of his smoothie, then replied, "Couple weeks ago."

"Do you know what caused the rift?"

"Well," he hesitated. "I wasn't supposed to overhear, but I was in the car after dropping the senator off at home when Mr. Slade roared up in that expensive toy. His daddy wasn't happy about it. 'Who do you think is going to pay for that?' the senator demanded. 'You will,' Slade answered. 'Oh, no, I won't,' said the senator. 'Then Grandma and Grandpa Fowler will,' the kid said smugly. 'Over my dead body,' shouted the senator. 'And from this day forward, don't ever ask me for money. You understand?'"

Clarence hesitated as though he'd already said too much.

"What happened then?" I prompted.

He shrugged. "Took the car around to the garage. But haven't heard 'em talk since." He polished off his drink, obviously finished with his story.

A moment later, a nondescript sedan pulled into the lot. I watched as it backed into a space. A man and woman got out and walked toward the shop where we sat.

Clarence stiffened. "Press," he whispered. "Stay here. I'll create a diversion so you can talk to Miz Fowler."

"Why are you doing this?" I asked.

"Let's just say there's some things happenin' I'm not at liberty to discuss. Besides, she wants to talk to you."

He got up and started out. I slurped the last of my smoothie and watched as he folded himself into the Mercedes and pulled up in front of the salon. I casually left the store as the two reporters reversed course and ran for their car.

Clarence got out of the Mercedes and entered the shop. A few seconds later, he emerged with a woman shielded by his coat. He opened the back door, helped her in, then drove off quickly. The reporters followed.

As I entered the beauty parlor, a heavyset islander in a flowered *muumuu* blocked my way.

"What you want here?" she asked.

"Please tell Mrs. Fowler that Agapé Jones would like to speak with her. She'll understand." I was hoping she was still there and Clarence had taken someone else with him.

The lady pushed through a beaded curtain to a back room, only to reappear shortly.

"Follow me," she directed.

She led the way through a second large room where ladies were seated in styling chairs and standing behind them. They all eyed me suspiciously. I was definitely out of my element.

Finally, in a third room, the woman I had seen in the family portraits waited.

Keilani Fowler looked frail and exhausted. But she held out her hand and took mine in a firm grip. "Mr. Jones, *aloha*. It's nice to finally meet you. Bob said you were on the other side of the island and wouldn't come for a few days."

What is it Bob doesn't want me to know? I thought, but said, "I'm happy to meet you, Mrs. Fowler."

"Please, call me Keilani." She gestured to the chair opposite her.

"Thank you for seeing me," I said as I took a seat. "I hope you'll be able to help with my investigation."

"I'll do anything I can to find out what happened to my son." Shadows surrounded her eyes, and she looked haunted. While on the force, I'd seen enough relatives of victims to recognize the look.

"When was the last time you saw Philip?" I asked as gently as I could.

"A week ago Sunday," she answered quickly. "He and Nicki came to dinner. It had been much too long. He'd been in California for Father's Day, so we celebrated late." I saw pools forming in her eyes, but they didn't spill over.

"How did he seem?"

She shrugged. "He was excited about starting graduate school at Scripps. He got his BS in marine biology from UH in May. I can't believe that was only six weeks ago." She shook her head, then met my eyes. "He wanted to study oceanography and save the world."

"How did you feel about his leaving Hawaii?"

"I didn't like it. You see, Mr. Jones—"

"Agapé," I corrected.

"Agapé," she repeated, then continued. "My husband, Tom, comes from a famous political family in California. His father and grandfather were in the state assembly, and a great-uncle was governor. Tom's brothers had political ambitions, too. As the third son, he decided to move away so he wouldn't have to compete with them. That's why he came to Hawaii."

"But if there's family in California—" I began. She held up her hand to stop me.

"The Fowlers are rich, powerful, overwhelming. They were mad because Tom moved here, and even angrier when he married me. They'd already selected his future wife. But he had other ideas."

She paused and a hint of a smile passed over her lips, but it never reached her eyes.

"I had just graduated from Sacred Hearts Academy and was spending the summer in Hale'iwa. Tom was campaigning and made an appearance there. From the moment I shook his hand, I knew he was the one. He apparently felt the same way since he called the next day. We were married less than six months later."

"That was pretty sudden, wasn't it?" I asked.

She chuckled, but there was no humor in it. "It was for his family. They didn't come. The wedding was on the beach, Hawaiian style, with a big luau afterward. You may have seen the photo when you were at the house."

I nodded. "The one in the entry, right?"

"Yes. We were very happy. A month later, Tom's parents reconsidered and surprised us with a big reception in San Francisco. I was overwhelmed by all the people. And I met the woman his folks wanted him to marry. She was blonde and tall and elegant—everything I wasn't. But I learned quickly what it meant to be a politician's wife. By the end of the evening, my mouth ached from smiling. The week in California seemed endless. I couldn't wait to get back to Oahu."

"I don't blame you."

She continued as if I hadn't spoken, remembering, her eyes drifting to a place near the ceiling. "Nearly three years later, my Koma was born. I wanted to give him a Hawaiian name, but Tom insisted the baby be called Thomas Slade Fowler, Jr., after himself. In order to avoid confusion, we've always used his middle name."

Ah, so this is Slade.

She glanced down at her hands, clasped in her lap. "I lost one baby before Koma, and three more after him. But we were determined not to have an only child. Six years later, Pilipo was born. I'm the only one who uses his Hawaiian name. Tom's grandfather had just died, so our second son became Philip, after him. Our family was complete, and life was wonderful."

She looked at me and smiled weakly at the memory. I remembered the other photo I'd seen in the house. It showed a happy family.

She continued. It was like 'talk story,' and I didn't want

to interrupt since I thought she might reveal something significant.

"Koma reached his teens, and Tom became very harsh with him. He would be the next Fowler in politics. I knew my son wasn't like his father, but no one listened. No matter what he did, it wasn't good enough. I'm afraid he reacted by teasing his little brother."

I nodded. I remember being teased by my older sister. I figured Philip was enough younger to make an easy target.

"Pilipo was blond like his father; Koma was dark like me. He called Pilipo his *haole* brother. That means 'foreigner'."

She glanced at me to see if I understood. Of course, I did. I was one, too.

She nodded when she saw recognition. "But, Agapé, you must understand. My Koma is a good boy."

There was a spark in her eyes I hadn't yet seen.

"He just didn't want to become a politician like his daddy. And it didn't help that his younger brother was better at everything. Pilipo was a good student, a natural athlete, and a wonderful person. He was my angel." She paused, then whispered, "And now he is one in heaven."

She took a long shuddering breath, then continued, "I'd been able to protect him here. The Fowlers were focused on Koma, so they ignored my younger son. But when they realized Koma wouldn't do as they wished, they began to work on Pilipo. They wanted him near them in California where they could influence him. Don't you see?"

I nodded. The Philip everyone described would have

been a perfect candidate. He was handsome and likeable and, from all accounts, charming.

"But he loved the ocean. My father taught both the boys to surf. Koma was good but Pilipo was outstanding. My baby adored the sea and every creature in it. It's such a loss…"

I thought I might have to find a tissue, but she straightened and stared at me intently.

"They've taken one of my sons. They can't have the other. Some reporters think Koma had something to do with it, but I know he didn't. Mr. Jones, you have to prove it."

It was the plea of a mother for her remaining child. But something about her intensity convinced me she believed completely in Slade's innocence.

I hoped she was right. "I'll do my best," I promised.

"Your word is enough," she said and took my hand as I stood.

I hope I won't let her down.

As we walked out of the back room, I noticed the Mercedes parked in front with a familiar-looking fellow leaning against it. As soon as he saw Keilani, he moved to open the back door.

"Thank you again, Mr. Jones," she said as she took my hand.

"It's Agapé, remember. And I'll do my best for you."

"That's all we can ask," she said. And then she was out the door and into the car. Clarence gave me a quick nod, then went around and drove off.

The large Hawaiian woman was still watching me intently, so I figured I'd better go, too. Besides, I was getting hungry. It was past one o'clock and all I'd had all day was fruit—if you didn't count the sherbet.

I decided to find a drive-through before going back to the other side of the island.

I don't know Kailua very well, so I was making circles around the area, looking for a fast food place when I spotted a Lamborghini. A red one. With black stripes.

Chapter 15: Chasing Slade

Slade's car (at least I assumed it was his car from Clarence's description) was parked in front of a five-story building with the name 'Shary, Taylor & Rugh' in large letters on the marquee sign. I knew that name. I'd see it in news articles on the North Shore Development fight. They were one of the companies attempting to build on the property adjoining the Turtle Bay Resort. I also remembered something about high-rise condos and a commercial complex.

What's Slade doing here? Clarence saw him before eleven o'clock. It's nearly one. Has he been here the whole time? And if not, where?

I'd passed the entrance before I noticed the car, so I drove around the corner and found another driveway. I made my way to a shady spot in the row nearest the exit and backed in. Then I rolled down the windows and enjoyed the soft breeze while waiting for the young man himself to appear.

Out of habit, I scanned the lot and noticed a white Toyota Prius with two men sitting in it. They could have been employees taking a late lunch, but I doubted it. They weren't talking, just concentrating on the building entrance.

While I waited, I realized that I hadn't really asked Keilani many questions. I had just let her talk. She seemed to need a chance to share her feelings. I just hoped that I'd get another opportunity with her after all the ceremonies were over tomorrow.

I pulled out my notebook and scribbled a few things. I also noticed the only items left from my previous night's entries were:

Call Watanabe – updates?
Ask Nicki again – What time did she see Philip last? Where? What mood had he been in? Did he say where he planned to go that Tuesday?

I didn't feel comfortable talking to Masa in the car, and Nicki was at work. Those two items would have to wait.

I added some notes from my conversations with Clarence and Keilani, all the while keeping an eye on the red sports car. I hoped the guys in the white car would think I was making notes for a meeting.

I hadn't been there more than five minutes when someone I readily identified as Slade Fowler emerged through the double glass front doors. Another man in a suit followed him out. They were shouting at each other, but I couldn't hear what they were saying.

Slade jumped into his car and roared off. I started mine.

So did the guys in the Prius. They were closer to the exit. I followed, allowing a small distance. I don't think they noticed me. They seemed intent on keeping up with the Lamborghini.

All of us were traveling too fast for traffic on the local streets, and Slade seemed determined to lose his tail. He zipped in and out, passing other cars on the way. The Prius tried to keep up while not drawing too much unwanted attention. So did I.

At the third signal, he squeaked through on a late yellow. (My wife would have called it 'pink.') We had to stop. There was cross traffic.

When the light changed, the Prius sped up, but Slade was long gone. I decided to follow the white car, matching its speed and wondering, *Who are these guys? Are they press, developers, cops or…*

They pulled into a shopping center parking lot and turned around. I continued past and made a U-turn at the next signal. There were three cars between us as we headed back towards Kailua.

The Prius turned onto the Pali Highway, along with two of the cars I was using as cover. I eased from lane to lane on the way back over the hill, always staying at a discreet distance and keeping a car or two between us. Just like a typical tourist.

The white car made an unexpected move and turned toward Honolulu. I was in the wrong lane to follow.

Damn, missed the turn. Never catch them now. You're really out of practice, Jones. Wonder who they were.

It was nearly two o'clock by the time I got back to Hale'iwa. I was starving by then, so I grabbed a fast burger and diet soda. I drove toward the beach park where I intended to call Watanabe, eating the burger on the way. However, on impulse, I turned into the parking lot of Typhoon Tommy's.

There were no spots, so I kept going to the back of the building. A beat-up old car, with lots of rust and faded paint, and a shiny new van were next to the warehouse. I still had the disposable camera in the Cobalt and wanted to get prints to take home to Gerry. I thought I might be able to take some photos of the shop to show Mal with the last few shots left in the camera.

I threw my empty burger wrapper into a can outside and entered through the open doorway next to the closed garage-type, roll-up door.

Inside, florescent fixtures suspended from the high, corrugated sheet metal ceiling lit the large space. Along the right-hand wall were completed boards, lying one above the other, separated by wooden dowels. To the left were cartons and other packaging material. Some boxes appeared to be sealed and addressed for shipping.

The sound of voices came from the next room.

I looked inside and saw two people, one in a wheelchair. I knocked on the doorframe. They looked up.

I thought I was in a time warp when the standing one turned around. He was tall and lanky with white-blond dreadlocks. He resembled Sean Penn in *Fast Times at Ridgemont High*. The image was reinforced when he opened his mouth.

"Yeah, man. Like whadda ya' want?" He seemed surprised to see me there. I guessed this was Wacko. His speech was a little slurred, but it could have been an affectation.

"My name's Agapé Jones," I began. "Jake said he'd design and build a surfboard for my grandson. I wondered if I could take a few pictures here in the shop so I could tell the kid all about how it was made. I'd like to get a couple of you, too, if you'll be working on it. I'd be something of a hero. So would you."

"Cool, dude," said the Sean Penn look-alike.

The younger guy in the wheelchair had spun around. He appeared to be in his late twenties, thin but with well-developed arms. He had dark eyes and long greasy-looking brown hair. I assumed this was Jamie Aiku-Howe, from Jake's description. He gave me a surly look but said nothing.

"Hey, Jay, did Jake, like, tag a blank this mornin'? Maybe it's this guy's."

Jamie shrugged and mumbled, "Don't know."

"All right, man. C'mon back and we'll check it out."

"Hey, Wacko," Jamie called after us. "Just don't mess up my stuff."

Wacko even laughed like the Jeff Spicoli character.

Fast Times wasn't a movie I'd ever have chosen to see, but my son, Martin, loved it and insisted I watch it with him, several times. I really couldn't understand the appeal of a lot of the humor, but I'll never forget that character. Now I felt I was meeting him in person.

"No worries, man," Wacko tossed over his shoulder as he

led the way farther into the shop. Jamie followed. I tagged along.

I had other things to do, but it was too good an opportunity to pass up. Heck, any chance to impress Mal was worth taking.

Jamie grunted and I turned to see his wheelchair enter the first opening.

The next one was covered by plastic strips, the kind I'd seen in butcher shops which obscured everything behind them. I started toward the doorway.

"Not that way, man," Wacko warned. "That's Cho's glossin' room where he does the final glass coat. It's a clean room. He don't want nothin' messin' up his finish."

The smell of bleach met my nose.

I followed Wacko down the corridor toward the rear of the building. On the way, we passed several additional rooms where surfboards seemed to be in various stages of completion.

"This is my shapin' bay," he announced proudly, pointing to the last door on the right. "I got 'The Machine.' Ain't she a beaut?"

In the middle of the room stood a large metal monstrosity half-buried in some sort of dust that resembled dirty snow. It looked like a cross between an MRI machine and a Shopsmith. There was a hole in the middle where, I assumed, the surfboards went. I could see saw blades, like sharks' teeth, protruding into the space.

"I make stock boards for the stores. See, I dial in the size and shape, shove a blank in here and out it pops. I just have to smooth and clean up the rails and check for defects. I can do like eight, maybe ten boards an hour. Jake's old school, works by hand. Even with his cool custom power planers from the mainland, he can only do two maybe three blanks, max."

"Very impressive," I commented and received a toothy smile in return.

"Jake's storeroom and bay're back here." He indicated the last room at the end of the hall.

We entered a smaller space. Fluorescent lights came on when he flipped the switch. I noticed a doorway to the right. Wacko walked to the back wall where what I assumed were surfboard blanks stood upright, separated by wooden dowels. Each had a tag taped to it.

He checked several before asking, "Jones the name?"

"That's right," I answered.

He pulled out a ten-foot long, two-foot wide, and four-inch thick chunk of white foam with a piece of wood running down the center, and set it across a pair of sawhorses in the center of the room.

So that's a blank.

"Cool," he said as he stepped back to admire it. "It already has the wood stringer in it, but it's really old school polyurethane. I have to cut my foam and glue the stringers, but mine are stronger and, like, don't show dings, ya know."

"Dings?" I questioned.

"Yeah, man, scratches, dents. You get 'em if you get

rammed by another board."

"Does that happen often?" I was sure I wouldn't tell Gerry about that. She'd worry.

"Yeah. Everybody gets 'em sooner or later. Or you could, like, hit a rock or coral, or just drop it." Then he snort-laughed again.

"Would it be okay if you took a picture of me standing next to it so I could show my grandson the beginning of his board?"

"Sure, man, no problemo," he said.

I handed him the camera and stood behind the big form. "This looks awfully long for Mal. I mean, he's only five-foot seven."

Wacko laughed again. "That's why we shape 'em. When Jake's through, this'll be one-of-a kind, just right for the kid, swear."

I noticed how neat the room was. "Jake really keeps things tidy," I observed.

"Yeah," Wacko said as he handed me back the camera. "He always says, 'Got to stay ahead of the mess.' But he only does a few boards at a time, man. I do lots more, ya know?"

He sounded a little defensive, so I nodded, but didn't think it required an answer. I remembered the big piles of debris I'd seen on the floor and all around Wacko's machine and against the walls.

"Do you think Jake would let me watch him work on the board?"

"Sure man. He always likes to show off those antique

power planers of his 'cause Skill hasn't made 'em since eighty-eight. Jake swears by 'em." Wacko shrugged. "Whatever."

"I hope he'll let me know when the time comes. I'd like to get pictures of the whole process."

"I'll tell him, man," Wacko said.

I wasn't sure if he'd remember, but at least I'd made the attempt.

"How long will it take him to finish?" I asked as I followed Wacko back down the hall.

He shrugged. "Couple weeks. Maybe more."

As we passed Wacko's room, I asked, "Could I take a picture of the machine? I'm sure Mal would be impressed."

"Sure, man," he answered.

"Would you pose next to it? That'll give him an idea of how big it is."

"Cool."

I snapped off a couple of shots from different angles to finish the camera.

"I don't have time now, but maybe I can get some showing you actually making boards when I come to watch Jake work."

He grinned.

We reached the front of the shop without seeing Jamie again. I guessed he was working or hiding.

"Thanks for the tour." I shook Wacko's hand.

"Catch you later, man," Wacko said as he loped off.

I looked at my watch. *Nearly three. Time to make some calls, then try to see Nicki.*

Chapter 16: Dinner With Nicki

I'd just gotten into the car when the theme from *Jaws* thumped in my pocket.

"Jones here," I answered.

"Agapé, it's Duke."

I coughed twice, then said, "Good to hear from you."

"Oh, yeah. Call me back when you get a chance."

"Will do."

I was glad he remembered our signal that I wasn't free to take his call.

I started the engine, drove to Hale'iwa Road, then turned into Hale'iwa Ali'i Beach Park. There were a few more people around this afternoon, so I parked, walked to a spot away from the crowd, and punched in Duke's speed-dial number.

"I'm back," I said when he answered.

"No eavesdroppers?"

"Not that I know of."

"We finally got the tox report back on the junk in Philip

Fowler's ears and nose. It appears to be polystyrene dust. It's pretty strange."

"Sounds like it to me," I agreed and made a note of it.

Polystyrene dust in Philip's ears, nose

For a second, I thought of the piles of dirty 'snow' I'd just seen in the surfboard shop. But Wacko had said Mal's blank was polyurethane. Still, I intended to do more checking.

"Does Watanabe know?" I asked, since I planned to phone him next.

"Sure. I contacted him first."

I wonder if he'll tell me about this when I talk to him.

"Have you found out anything new?" Duke asked.

"I finally met Keilani Fowler. She's sure her other son, Slade, isn't involved in any way. But then I saw him coming out of Shary, Taylor, & Rugh. Don't know what that connection's about."

"That's one of the big players trying to build on the North Shore, isn't it?"

"Yeah. Their last try was blocked, but they're not giving up." Mano had mentioned the name in connection with one of his protests, and I'd also heard it on the news.

"I'll see what I can find out from here," Duke said.

"Thanks. By the way, were you able to trace the plate on the black Nissan?"

"The registration's a little murky, but it seems to belong

to the local PD in that area."

Hmmm. Maybe the senator isn't completely paranoid about the local police. Is Nicki being watched? Was Philip?

I added the information to my notebook.

"Thanks. I'll keep that in mind," I told him.

"Take care and let me know if you need anything."

"Will do."

I punched in Watanabe's number.

"Detective Watanabe," he answered.

"Masa, it's Agapé Jones."

"Good afternoon, Mr. Jones. What can I do for you?"

"I just wanted to touch base and find out if you've uncovered anything new."

"Nothing at all, I'm afraid."

I wish I knew why he's not being completely candid with me.

"What about you?" he continued.

"I talked to Mrs. Fowler but wasn't able to get any useful information from her. I'd still like to talk to Slade Fowler, but I'm discovering he's pretty hard to pin down."

"Umm," he replied. I didn't know whether he was agreeing with me or just letting me know he was still on the line.

I debated mentioning the black Nissan but decided I'd wait a little longer. I also decided not to say anything about the white Prius following Slade. For all I knew, it could have been press like the folks stalking Mrs. Fowler.

"I hear you will be participating in the paddle-out tomorrow."

He surprised me with that statement. "Yes. I'll be in an

outrigger with a local club. How did you know?"

"Security is very high for the event," he answered. It made sense in a way, but his interest felt personal. I wondered if he saw me as a threat or an ally.

"Will you be there tomorrow?" I asked.

"I will be around," he replied. I wasn't sure what that meant, either.

"Then I'll probably see you." I figured I'd take it at face value, or at least appear to.

"Thank you for calling, Mr. Jones. Please let me know if you learn anything important."

"I will," I said, and I meant it. Although he wasn't being completely forthright with me, he was the local authority, and he had jurisdiction.

It was after three-thirty, and Nicki should be home. I decided to see if she'd give me a little more time. I was sorry to ask since she was probably involved with all the events scheduled for the next day, but Lovey was right. She was the last person known to have seen Philip alive, so she was the place to start.

Her car was in the driveway, so I pulled up in front. The black Nissan was gone—for the moment. There was no sign of the neighbors.

I knocked, and she answered quickly. She'd already changed out of her work clothes into a pair of shorts and a tank top.

"I'm sorry to bother you," I began. "But would you do me a favor?"

She hesitated a moment, then said, "If I can."

"I haven't had a nice restaurant meal since I got here, and I really hate to eat alone. Since I'm on expenses, I wondered if you'd consider having an early dinner with me at Jameson's. I've heard a lot about it and would like to try it before I leave."

It was an impulsive request. I'd passed the restaurant every time I traveled back and forth to Turtle Bay, and I had heard the food was good. So it wasn't untrue, exactly.

"Uh—sure, I guess," she answered. "But I'm not really dressed for dinner."

I laughed. "Neither am I, but I understand there's no dress code, and we're not into the dinner hour yet."

She gave me a half-smile. "Well, I did skip lunch, so I guess I could."

"Great. Thanks," I said before she could change her mind. I wasn't too hungry after the burger I'd eaten. But I needed time to talk to her, and a relaxed meal might just allow the opportunity.

She left for a moment, and returned with a small purse. After locking up, she followed me to the car. I opened her door for her. She seemed a little surprised, although I'd done the same thing the last time we ate 'the best burgers on Oahu, maybe in the whole world'. Between Lovey and Gerry, I'd finally figured out that women like those little touches of gentlemanly behavior. Nicki, it seemed, was no exception.

When we arrived at the restaurant, we were immediately escorted to a table near the water. The place was nearly deserted since it was late for the lunch crowd and not yet dinner time. That suited my purposes.

The waiter arrived with menus and asked about our beverages.

"Wine?" I asked.

"I don't think so," she answered.

We ordered iced teas instead. Gerry would like that. I was looking forward to a nice glass of the good stuff with her when I got back home to Maui.

While we waited, we looked at the menus.

"Would you like an appetizer?" I asked.

"I'd rather just order an entrée if it's okay with you," she answered. "I just realized I'm hungry. Oh, but go ahead if you want."

"I don't need one," I replied as the waiter appeared to take our orders.

Nicki selected the grilled crab and shrimp melt sandwich. It sounded really good, but since I wasn't too hungry, I settled on the shrimp stir fry.

I'll have to remember to tell Gerry about this meal and skip over the burger I had for lunch.

"Thanks for joining me," I said.

"I appreciate the distraction," she replied. "Tomorrow will be a busy and emotional day, I'm afraid." The sadness had returned to her face.

"I wish I could get to the church service," I said. "But I was asked to paddle with a local canoe club here. There probably won't be time to do both."

"No. Especially with the traffic coming from Honolulu."

She had a thoughtful expression on her face. Then she looked at me. "Thank you for taking part. I appreciate it, and I know the family will as well."

"You're close to the family?" This was the opening I'd waited for.

"Many of the *ali'i* families still feel a bond. Since I was going to marry Phil..." Her voice dropped off, but after a moment she straightened and continued, "...they treated me as part of their family. I still feel the same way about them." As she spoke, she twisted the ring on her finger.

"I've been trying to contact Slade Fowler. Do you think he knows anything about what happened to Philip?"

She looked genuinely stunned that I would suggest such a thing. "No way. Slade watched out for Phil and was very proud of him."

"But I heard that he teased him and called him a *haole*."

She smiled faintly. "Oh, he did. But Slade was the only one who could call him that. If someone else tried it, Slade would have beaten him up. And he had a reputation for fighting—and winning—so the others usually backed off."

Maybe Keilani's trust in Slade isn't so misplaced after all.

"How did Philip feel about Slade?"

For a second she frowned, then answered, "Although they were very different in some ways, they genuinely loved each other. Phil looked up to his big brother. I sometimes thought Phil realized that Slade's rebellion meant that he didn't have to rebel. He often told me how sorry he'd felt for his brother since the senator put so much pressure on him to follow in his footsteps." She shook her head. "It's no wonder he fought back."

The waiter brought our meals, and we began to eat but continued talking. The relationship between the brothers was something I needed to find out about, and I didn't want to waste the opportunity.

"When did the pressure switch from Slade to Philip?"

She'd previously told me of her fears about Philip being overwhelmed by the political Fowler grandparents in California.

She looked thoughtful as she took a bite of her sandwich followed by a sip of her tea. "I guess they finally gave up on Slade about the time Phil started college. I remember him telling me his father had begun completely ignoring Slade and had started to pressure him about a career in politics when we first met. I know his father's insistence grew stronger in the last couple of years, especially when he found out Phil was considering going to grad school in California."

As she talked, she'd stopped eating and lowered her eyes.

"How did Slade feel about no longer being the heir apparent?" I asked.

She shook her head again. "I'm not sure. On one hand, I think he was relieved. But on the other hand, he'd gone from being under the microscope and the center of attention twenty-four/seven to being ignored. He seemed confused and without direction. Then he started behaving even more recklessly. I felt it was to regain some of his dad's attention. But that was just my opinion."

Her brow furrowed again.

Then she continued. "I've been so upset and guilty about the argument we had afterward that I'd all but forgotten... When Phil came home last week, he said he was worried about Slade. Said he had to find him."

"Did he say why?"

She seemed distracted. "I keep wondering if we hadn't had the fight, maybe he'd still be alive."

"Why did Philip need to find Slade?" *Get her back to the story, Jones. This could be important.*

"Phil said he'd stopped by to see his folks but they weren't home. As he was leaving, he overheard Bob Hillman talking to someone on the phone. He said something like, 'We need to take care of the kid. Slade isn't coming through, and it cost us enough. We'll have to teach him a lesson.' Phil got out of the house before Bob knew he was there, at least he thought he had."

She blanched and her eyes grew wide.

"Oh my God, you don't think someone killed Phil as a warning to Slade, do you?' she asked.

That was exactly what I thought, but I wouldn't commit. "Could be," I answered. "Who does Bob know who'd threaten Slade?"

"That's easy. North Shore developers. I've heard rumors that he was getting paid to influence the senator. Maybe they paid Slade, too. I really don't trust Bob Hillman."

I didn't either. Hadn't for quite some time. But I tried to keep my face passive. All I could think of was seeing Slade at

Shary, Taylor, and Rugh just a few hours earlier. And he was clearly arguing with someone. *There must be a connection.*

"If Philip left to look for his brother, where would he have gone?" I asked.

Nicki took time to think before answering. "I don't know for sure, but Slade used to stop by the surfboard factory when he was in this area. At least at first. Lately, though, he seemed to lose interest, as his father kept reminding him."

"What do you mean?"

"Recently the senator seemed to take every opportunity to point out to Slade that he'd invested in the business so Slade would have something to keep him busy, but Slade never got involved."

It was obvious, even to me and I didn't know the guy, that Philip was the one interested in surfing, not Slade. Keilani mentioned that her father had taught both boys when they were younger. But Philip had the drive to excel in the sport. "Why would Senator Fowler assume that Slade would want to be part of a surfboard manufacturing venture?"

She shook her head. "Slade's had momentary enthusiasm for lots of different things. Phil said that in high school he decided to take guitar lessons, but when he found out he'd have to practice to get good, he gave it up. Same with tennis. He's a natural athlete like Phil and played well enough. But his dad wanted him to be the best. Slade wasn't competitive. So instead of playing for fun, he just quit. That's sort of been the pattern of his life so far. He seems to have a short attention span."

Given the pressure to please his father, I must say I felt a little sorry for Slade. Maybe Keilani's faith in her remaining son had some merit.

"So, do you think Philip might have gone to Liquid Excitement looking for Slade?"

"Maybe. But there are lots of other places he might have been."

I decided to try a different tack. "If you'd been the one looking for Slade, where would you have looked? Did he have any friends? Any regular hangouts?"

"Phil was the social one, even though he was quiet. He had lots of good friends, and not just surfers. Slade was a loner. I suspect he's very sensitive and thoughtful. Phil always said his dad had wounded Slade, but Slade would never have let his father know. Instead, he mouthed off and acted out."

I could see she seemed to care about both of the brothers.

We finished our meal in relative silence, each of us in our own thoughts.

As I left her at her door some time later I said, "If you think of anything—anything at all that could be important—please contact me." I gave her my cell number but didn't expect to hear from her, at least not until after all the events of the next day.

Chapter 17: Shaping Mal's Board

After dropping Nicki off, I'd stopped by Foodland to pick up another papaya to go with my remaining banana. I asked about getting prints from my disposable camera. They told me Del's Camera had quick developing.

It took me a while to locate the shop, and by the time I did, it was too late to get the pictures the same day. I bought another disposable, this time a water-resistant one, and left the first. I'd have to remember to pick up the prints in the morning.

On the way back to the hotel, I drove past the boat dock. The big yacht was still there, but it looked deserted. I wasn't surprised. I figured the senator was at home with his family, preparing for the big day. And Terry was probably at his side.

I got to the room about seven-thirty and tried to call Gerry. There was no answer, so I turned on the TV. At home, I usually catch the news and watch a couple of shows before going to sleep. But I couldn't concentrate.

I tried calling again about eight-thirty, and then at nine.

Still no answer.

It seemed a little strange for her to be out that late when she had class the next day, but I hoped she was enjoying herself.

I watched another mindless show until ten. Then I turned off the light and tried to get to sleep. But I hadn't said goodnight to my wife. It's been part of our nighttime routine for as long as we've been married—and that's most of my life.

I gave up at around ten-twenty and tried one more call. This time, Gerry picked up.

"Hi, honey," I said.

"I'm glad you called," she answered. "I was afraid I wouldn't be able to get to sleep without hearing your voice, and I thought it was too late to call you."

I chuckled. "I've been trying to sleep, but I needed to say goodnight."

She laughed with me. "Aren't we old creatures of habit?"

"Yeah, but it's a nice habit. The only thing missing is our goodnight kiss. Oh, and the one first thing in the morning."

"I miss you. I had dinner with Chuck and Maggie at that new Italian restaurant we've been talking about trying."

"How was it?"

"Well, I think we'll stick with the old standbys. This one was pretty pricey and not great. If we want to splurge, we'll go to Longhi's."

"So you had a late dinner, huh?" I asked.

"No. Actually we had an early one and then went to see that new romantic comedy I talked about. You aren't terribly fond of those, and Chuck enjoys them."

"How was it?" I asked but was secretly happy that I didn't have to go.

"Not worth the price of the ticket. You can catch it when it comes on TV."

"Great."

"What did you have for dinner?" she asked.

"I took a pretty young Hawaiian girl out for a nice meal near the ocean."

"Oh really? Young, was she? And pretty?"

I laughed. "Yes, but she was also the fiancée of the young man who was killed. I was doing a little investigating."

"Well, just finish investigating and come home. I thought you weren't going to get too involved. Sounds as though you're back in the middle."

"Uh, just going over territory the locals have already covered."

"And did you find out anything?"

"Maybe. I'll pass along what I learned tomorrow. Don't know if it's news to them."

"See that you let them do the real work. And, honey, please be careful. I miss you. Heck, I can't even get to sleep without saying goodnight to you."

"I know. I have the same problem. But I'll be home soon. Meantime, sleep well. I love you."

I hoped I would get home soon, but at the moment I didn't see how unless I just gave up. And I don't do that.

* * * *

I woke up early and couldn't get back to sleep. Last night's conversation with Nicki still replayed in my mind. I needed to talk to Slade. But I couldn't dwell on him because today would be busy and I couldn't follow up until at least after the luau.

After I finished my PT, I showered, dressed, and decided to head for Hali'ewa. I'd get breakfast there. The papaya and banana didn't appeal to me as much in the light of day as they had the night before at the store.

When I passed Typhoon Tommy's, I noticed a newer black truck parked at the shop out back. I'd seen Jamie and Wacko's vehicles, and the truck wasn't theirs. I didn't know what Cho drove, but I guessed the truck belonged to Jake. On impulse, I pulled in next to it in the deserted dirt lot. Tommy's wouldn't be open for a couple of hours.

The large garage-style door was closed. I nearly turned to leave when I noticed the other door ajar. Since it was still early, I wondered if it was supposed to be open.

I peered inside. The corridor lights were on but the rooms were dark. I could hear the sound of a power tool coming from far down the hallway.

"Hello," I called, but got no response. I started past the room holding Wacko's big machine. The sound stopped.

"Hello," I tried again. "Anyone here?"

A head appeared around the far doorway. It was Jake. He looked surprised, and then recognition crossed his face.

"Jones, isn't it?" he asked. "How'd you get in here?"

"The door wasn't closed. I just walked in," I explained.

"The main door?"

"Yes."

"I've been after Wacko to get that latch fixed for weeks. It's supposed to shut automatically, but sometimes it doesn't catch. Thought I'd slammed it hard enough, but I guess not."

"You remembered my name."

"I always remember a client, especially when they've ordered a custom board," he said. "The blank I ordered arrived. I could shape it now if you'd like to watch."

"That would be great," I replied, although my stomach gave a slight protest. I hadn't had breakfast or any coffee yet.

"Follow me," he said.

"Wacko showed me the blank yesterday. It looks really big for a kid Mal's size," I told him as I entered.

"Blanks only come in a couple of basic sizes," he explained. "It's a little like sculpting from a block of stone. The shaper knows the board's in there somewhere. It's my job to free it."

We walked through the room where Wacko had shown me the blank and entered Jake's small shaping room next door. It was about ten feet wide and fifteen feet long. In the center, a white foam surfboard was placed on Y-shaped racks. Fluorescent lights were mounted about waist-high along each wall.

Jake carefully removed the board he'd been working on from the racks and placed it in the adjoining room. He returned and swept the floor, emptying the dustpan into a nearby bin.

"Kind of a habit I got into," he said. "Got to stay ahead of the mess."

I recalled Wacko quoting him. I also remembered the big piles of shavings I'd seen in Wacko's area. Jake probably wasn't too happy about that.

"I'll get your blank," he said and left the room.

He returned with the ten-foot long, two-foot wide, and four-inch thick plank I'd seen the day before.

"Mind if I take a few pictures of the process?" I asked, pulling the camera from my pocket. "I took a couple with Wacko yesterday."

"No flash pictures when I'm running the power planer. It could be a little dangerous if I got distracted. But any other time would be okay."

Jake placed the blank flat on top of the Y-shaped rack, measured for the length he wanted, and cut off each end with a hand saw. On the back wall of the shaping bay, hung from nails, were maybe twenty pieces of plywood and plastic sheets cut into curved shapes. Jake studied these carefully and then picked one.

"Templates," he explained. "Every good shaper develops an assortment. Some I've made myself, others, like this one I inherited from Jim Whyte, the man who taught me. He was the best in the area until he was in a car accident. He could still glass, though, and he was great at it. Worked here until a few months ago. Had a stroke, and his son took him back to the mainland. It was tough replacing him."

Tommy had told me a little about it.

While he was talking, he'd carefully laid the template he'd selected across the top of the blank, marking the place where it crossed the center stringer on the template. Next, he traced the curved outline with a pencil. Then he flipped the sheet over, aligned it, and marked a mirror image for the other side.

I clicked off a couple of photos during the process.

Jake returned the template carefully, almost reverently, to its place. Then, again with the hand saw, he cut along the pencil lines. It now began to look less like a foam box and more like one of those old wooden paddleboards I remembered seeing at the beach when I was a kid, the ones with the square sides. I'd always wanted to try one, but somehow it was never the right time.

"Better put on one of those masks." He motioned to several on a shelf as he reached for a power tool. "No pictures now, okay?"

"Got it," I answered.

He pulled on his own mask and began running the powerful machine along the side.

For the next half hour, I watched the artist at work. The square edges became rounded. The flat bottom and top were curved gracefully from nose to tail. I now saw the reason for the Y-shaped supports as he frequently flipped the board over, even standing it on its side in the notch of the Y to concentrate on getting the curves just right. Several times he paused to study the shape intently, then made slight adjustments. Finally, he removed his mask and stood back.

"That's about it," he said. "I left the rails a little thicker." He pointed to the side edges. "And put a slight vee in the bottom where the fin will attach. Should make it easier to paddle and catch waves—for a beginner."

"Thanks. I didn't know so much work went into making one of these."

"This is just the beginning," he said. "A fine sanding to remove any rough spots, and it will be ready for color and glassing. You going to get any special airbrushing or tape-offs?"

"Huh?"

"Do you want a pattern or design?"

"Hadn't thought about it. Maybe some striping would be nice." From my high school days, I knew about pin-striping. I figured it was similar with surfboards.

"Check with Wacko. He's got some samples and photos up front. I don't go in for the fancy stuff so much myself. But a young kid might. It doesn't make them ride any better."

He finished smoothing the board with sandpaper, marked his name and a number on the stringer, and entered the number, my name, and a description in a logbook on his shelf.

"I always mark down the customer and template I used in case they want another just like it," he said as he placed the finished product with the others against the wall.

"So, how long before it'll be ready?" I asked

"First, Jamie will do the final sanding. Then the blank needs to rest and breathe for a while before Cho glasses it. If Wacko airbrushes it, that has to dry. Then the fin box is cut in, and a base coat of polyester resin and fiberglass is applied and sanded. Any tape-offs or colors you want will be added and allowed to set. After that, Cho will apply the gloss coat. Jamie will do the final sanding, and Cho will polish it. In all, it should take about two weeks to complete, depending on the design you pick."

"I'm not planning on being on Oahu that long." I said, sorry that I'd miss some of the process.

He grinned. "We ship boards all over the world. The big shipment we're packing this week is going to Japan. We also ship all over the rest of Asia and to Australia, New Zealand, and even Ireland. Where do you live?"

It was on the tag and the order form, but I wasn't surprised he didn't remember.

"Maui."

"Piece o' cake. In fact, I go there all the time. I could bring it with me when it's finished, if that's okay."

"That would be great. Thanks again. I really appreciate this," I said, shaking his hand.

"Great doing business with you, Mr. Jones. Wacko can help you pick any designs, colors, or decals you think your grandson would like."

"How about some breakfast?" I suggested. "My treat."

"I'd love to, but I've got three more boards to shape this morning. And I need to be ready for the paddle-out later on."

"Okay, some other time then," I said. "By the way, is there a good breakfast place here in Hale'iwa?"

He looked thoughtful, then answered, "The Café

Hale'iwa's pretty good for breakfast. They have pancakes and stuff."

"Sounds like just the spot to me," I said and asked for directions.

He described the route. "It's not far," he added.

I thanked him again. As I turned to leave, he picked up the broom to prep the room for his next task.

On the way out, I spotted the piles of shavings in Wacko's area.

Jake keeps the shop neat. So why does he allow the mess in Wacko's area? Is Wacko so good at what he does that he doesn't have to follow the rules?

Something didn't quite add up, but I couldn't figure out exactly what it was. Besides, I was hungry. I decided to let the uncertainty lie awhile, at least until I'd had some coffee.

Chapter 18: Confrontation

I followed Jake's directions. The café was a little farther down Kam Highway than the burger place, but I found it easily. It was a surfer hangout, a small place with funky décor, just the kind of spot I really enjoy.

As he'd said, the food was great and at a good price. I ordered eggs and Portuguese sausage with fresh juice instead of the pancakes. I figured Gerry'd be happier about that—but not much. However, when the next table got their stack of banana ones, I had second thoughts. They only lasted a short while until my own breakfast arrived. Delicious, with lots of hot coffee.

I ate slowly, savoring the good flavors and thinking again about what Nicki had told me the night before. Slade's public image wasn't very good from what I'd heard. Yet she and Keilani both believed in him. Now I knew I had to meet him to find out for myself. I'm usually a pretty good judge of character. If something's off, I sense it. So far, Slade was my best suspect, but after talking with his mother and Nicki, I was starting to think he might not be such a great one after all. And that left me with nothing. At least, nothing with any substance. I had questions about the black Nissan, the local police, the North Shore developers, the surfboard shop, but not a thing I could really identify as significant.

Home looked better all the time. Frustration was becoming my best friend.

I thought of calling Duke, but what could I tell him? All I'd probably do is vent. I knew he'd listen, but he didn't need that.

I wished Lovey were here. I could always bounce ideas off her when she was alive. And, although I occasionally had conversations with her in my mind, she seemed to be particularly quiet this morning. I knew what she'd have said anyway. "Patience isn't your forte, son. Give it time, and keep your eyes and ears open." And she'd have been right.

I stopped by the camera store and picked up the pictures. I glanced through them in the car. The ones of the room were pretty good, at least good enough to show Gerry what she'd missed.

I smiled when I looked at the ones taken in the shop. In my mind, I rehearsed what I'd tell Mal about how his new board was made when I gave it to him. Boys—young men—of his age don't think older folks know much, so I hoped to impress him with my knowledge.

I slipped the photos back into the envelope and put them in the glove compartment.

I needed to walk off breakfast, so I headed the car back

toward Hale'iwa Beach Park. Preparations were well underway for the paddle-out and the events to follow. A news truck with satellite link was parked at the top of the hill, and I spotted a few police cars in the lot.

Too much activity and confusion. I'd rather walk somewhere quieter.

The marina didn't look quite as busy, so I turned at the sign for boat-launch parking and found an empty spot.

As I locked up and headed for the dock area, I saw two locals sitting on stools, repairing some fishing nets drying in the sun. They eyed me suspiciously, but neither rose or said anything as I passed.

Think I'll check out the senator's yacht. Maybe Terry's still on board.

As I approached the docks, I saw a familiar bearded figure coming toward me. He had a fishing rod slung over his shoulder and was lugging a plastic bucket. When he set it down, I saw four or five good-sized fish.

"Good morning, Tommy," I said, eyeing his catch. "Looks like you did okay out there today."

"Hi, Agapé. Sure did. I try to get out for dawn patrol a couple of times a week. 'Specially when the surf's down. Fishing's my other passion. But I usually toss back more than I keep." He laughed and leaned the pole against the railing.

He pointed at the line of boats. "That's my Boston Whaler down there, third from the end. She's a beaut. Gets me right to the good spots no matter what the weather. If you're around long enough, why don't you join me sometime?"

"I just might take you up on that," I said. When I was little, my dad used to take me fishing, just the two of us. The girls didn't get to go. It's one of my favorite memories of the man who died when I was twenty. "By the way, you seen any activity on the senator's yacht lately?"

"'Bout three weeks ago, there was a big party on board. Lit up half the marina. Since then, it's been quiet."

"I thought Terry might be there."

"I saw him around yesterday afternoon. He was with that classy blond. She's a real looker. Seen her on the yacht several times."

I must have looked puzzled.

"She's hard to miss. Don't often see high-maintenance women like her around here. Heck, Naomi never walked around with her nose in the air or looked down on the locals, and she has lots of money. But this one..." He shook his head.

I got the feeling he wasn't too fond of her. "Is she Terry's girlfriend?"

"Don't think so, not the way she bosses him around. Besides, uh, she usually seems to be hanging onto the senator."

I got the impression Tommy thought he might have said too much.

"None of my business anyhow," he added.

"Did you see anyone today?" I asked.

"Nope. Been quiet all morning. Better get these babies cleaned and filleted." He picked up the bucket and settled the pole back on his shoulder. "Toshi's probably got the shop open by now. We're closing down for the paddle-out. There won't be much business anyway with everyone going to the service. Now don't you forget, just give me a call and I'll take you fishin'."

"Thanks, I'll remember." I watched him carry his stuff toward the lot.

Tommy told me Jamie had a fishing boat, and Jake had described it. I checked my notes.

Jamie's Boat - 33 ft. Grady

None of the craft at the dock met that description.

Maybe he's out fishing, too.

I saw a large white catamaran yacht tied up. I spotted several *kahili* around the perimeter. I'd seen feather-topped *kahili* like these at the museum and knew they were standards used by Hawaiian royalty to signify their status, lineage, and family ties in the way European nobility use banners with coats of arms. I figured this catamaran would take the family out to spread the ashes. And once again, the sad waste of a young life struck me.

As appealing as the thought was of just giving up and going home to leave solving the case to the local authorities, I knew Lovey was right. Philip had come to me, and I had an obligation to continue investigating, not just for him but also for myself.

I checked the senator's yacht, but it was locked up tight.

About time I headed over to the canoe club anyway, while I might be able to find a parking spot, I said to myself as I turned toward the waiting Cobalt.

* * * *

I drove by the bridge where I'd met Doc Schwenck two days before. Even though I was early for the paddle-out, the lot was near capacity, and groups of people were already assembled along the harbor-front. I locked the car and headed toward the beached outrigger.

Before I got there, a bunch of locals started toward me.

"Hey, *haole*, what you doing here?" a big Hawaiian in black trunks asked. "We be watching. You hang around here couple days now. Not like tourist. We thinking you part of North Shore takeover. What you say, *haole*?"

Five of the group, all younger and easily stronger than me, formed a semi-circle, blocking my path. Their leader, the one who'd spoken, approached. He looked to be about six-foot-two and two-hundred-thirty pounds. He had a Hawaiian shoulder tattoo of a stylized sea turtle encircled by a breaking wave. Several of the others also sported shoulder, armband, or leg tattoos of Hawaiian design.

In my years with NYPD, I'd faced similar odds, but then I was in uniform, packing, and usually had backup on the way. *Wish I had the reassuring weight of my gun on my hip right now.*

I considered correcting their impression. I wasn't really a *haole* anyway. That means 'foreigner' or one who doesn't belong. Since we'd lived in Hawaii for a few years, we were now *kamaaina*—those who moved to Hawaii and had lived there awhile.

However, their menacing looks didn't seem to invite discussion.

Seeing all these big guys closing in, I recalled being outnumbered and called names in school. I grew up away from the city where there were few black families. I can remember being called ugly names and getting into fights when I tried to defend myself.

I'd come home battered and bloody, but of course I never told Lovey why.

"Son, you been fightin' again?" she'd ask with that disapproving frown.

I'd nod, but I never explained.

She'd clean me up and give me a lecture on ignoring the bullies.

But the names still hurt. Maybe they were part of the reason I decided to go into law enforcement—so I'd be able to defend others against the kind of bias I'd encountered.

I didn't like the quiver of fear running down my spine any more now than I did as a kid.

"Yo...Ekana," I heard a voice call from behind the group, pulling me out of my memories as they closed in. "That's no way to greet a brother."

Keola, canoe paddle in hand, pushed his way through the line to stand next to me.

"Agapé here is friend of Doc Schwenck's from over Maui-side. He be helping paddle outrigger three today."

Ekana's glare softened slightly and the group behind him visibly relaxed.

"That true? You say you friend of the Doc?" the leader asked, looking straight into my eyes.

"Sure, Schwenck and I go way back. Worked together with *Doctors Without Borders*." It was a small lie but sounded good. Besides, Gerry and I had done some fundraising for the organization back in New York.

"Well, if Keola say you okay, and Doc say you okay, that be good enough. Better watch out though, some on North Shore not so friendly as us." He patted my shoulder in a not-so-friendly way and nodded to his group. They moved away, and I breathed easier.

"Thanks, Keola," I said. "That was close. Glad you happened along."

"I saw them watch you get out of your car and thought there might be trouble. I came over fast as I could. Ekana's not a bad guy. He's had some run-ins with both the law and the developers lately. I'd steer clear of him and all the black trunks."

"Black trunks?"

"They patrol the North Shore and sometimes use fear, intimidation, and their fists to gain respect. They decide who rides what waves and punish outsiders who don't follow their rules. It's kind of like a North Shore Mafia."

"Now I'm really glad you came to my rescue. Thanks for the advice," I said.

Could this group have had something against Philip? Not

likely, since he was a local and ali'i. But still...

Before I had time to give it more thought, Doc and Naomi arrived with the rest of the team. I retrieved a *hoe* from the equipment box, and we slid the outrigger to the shoreline and waited for the paddle-out to start.

Chapter 19: Paddle-Out

"Agapé, here's your lei," Naomi said as she placed a fragrant string of plumeria around my neck and kissed me on the cheek.

She was wearing white orchids. Doc had on a lei like mine. She made her way to each team member and distributed the beautiful garlands.

We gathered around her as she gave instructions.

"We'll wait here with the other canoes and surfers until the big catamaran clears the harbor entrance. Then we'll all paddle out together. Remember, we need to get into the water without hurting anyone."

I was a little concerned since a crowd of hundreds of surfers and paddlers had assembled on the beach.

"We may want to wait for the surfers to get into the water before we start," Doc said. "They're anxious to be in the surf. After all, Philip was one of them. Our canoes take a bit more room."

His suggestion made sense.

I scanned the crowd and spotted Jake and Wacko with their boards. There was no sign of Jamie. And I hadn't ever met Cho, so I didn't know whether he was there or not.

Right then, we heard the noise of helicopters approaching.

"The family must be arriving from Honolulu," Naomi observed. And just as she said it, several long black limousines came into view. They turned into the boat launch area of the marina. I figured the family would board the big catamaran I'd spotted earlier.

Doc shaded his eyes and focused skyward. "Looks as though all the media outlets are here as well as the police."

I wasn't surprised. Several more TV trucks had arrived. There was no parking anywhere near the beach park, and I was glad I'd come early.

"Where did you park?" I asked. I didn't see his SUV anywhere.

He laughed. "It helps to be a local and know people. I'm in a friend's private spot about a block away. He dropped us off here because he's not planning on sticking around. Says he'll catch it all on the news tonight. Since he knows the family, he'll see them later in the week."

"Glad you made it," I responded.

Just then, we heard a conch blow from the other side of the jetty. A few seconds later, the big catamaran rounded the end. It picked up a little speed as it started out to sea. At the same time, the surfers hurried into the water and jumped on their boards.

Terry rushed up.

"Wasn't sure I'd make it," he huffed, out of breath. "It's been a madhouse. Even though the limo dropped me off at the corner, getting through the crowd was a challenge."

He retrieved his *hoe* and then jogged back. Everyone else appeared from wherever they'd been waiting.

"Let's go," Naomi announced.

We pushed the canoe into the water. Several others were doing the same.

When we were all in, Naomi called "*Ae*" and we responded with "*Ho.*" Slicing through the water felt familiar. We weren't going for speed, just moving toward the circle forming offshore. We turned the canoe so that it made part of an outer circle beyond the surfers in the middle.

Once we'd stopped paddling and were settled, I looked to my left toward the big catamaran. It had backed in to fill a gap in the ring of surfers. In addition to the senator and Keilani, Slade stood with his arm around Nicki. They looked very serious, and I felt compassion for both of them, imagining how emotional the day had already been. Next to the senator sat an older woman I took to be his mother. Actually she didn't look all that old with her unnaturally blond hair. Gerry would have called her 'well-preserved.' A man I assumed was the father, from his resemblance to Senator Fowler, stood behind the woman.

Everyone else was dressed in Hawaiian attire except these two. Both were in severe black suits.

The local *kahuna* stood in the center of the catamaran,

holding the conch. Next to him was another man in a robe who cradled a large calabash. I assumed he was the pastor of the church where the funeral had been held and the wooden vessel held Philip's ashes.

I nearly choked when the men moved apart and I spotted the two people who stood next to Mrs. Fowler. The couple, obviously her parents, looked very, very familiar. They should have, since I'd had dinner with them only a couple of nights earlier. Mano stood tall and straight in his crisply-pressed white pants and dark flowered shirt. Keilani held onto one of his arms while Malia held the other. I wondered if it was for physical stability or emotional strength—or both.

I didn't have much time to think about the older couple, however, because the drums started on the beach and the *kahuna* blew the conch again. Then the pastor handed him the calabash. Both stepped to the stern of the boat. The *kahuna* removed the lid and raised it high above as the sound of the drums intensified. Apparently there was some signal onshore, and the drums stopped suddenly.

The catamaran began to move slowly away from the circle, and the *kahuna* started to pour out the contents.

At the same time, the pastor began to speak. "And now, we return the mortal remains of Philip Fowler to the sea he loved. We know that he is not here but now dwells with his God and his ancestors where we will one day be reunited with him."

The ashes began to form a shiny silver path on the water. Those on the catamaran tossed their leis in the sea to join the ashes.

The *kahuna* lowered the calabash and began to sing the Hawaiian Benediction:

Ho`o nani ka Makua mau
Ke Keiki me ka Uhane no,
Ke Akua mau
Ho`o mai ka`i, pu,
Ko ke ia ao, ko ke la ao
Amene

The minister followed with the English version:

Praise God from whom all blessings flow.
Praise Him all creatures here below.
Praise Him above, ye heavenly hosts.
Praise Father, Son and Holy Ghost.

As if on queue, the surfers began tossing their leis into the center of the circle and splashing. Between the movement of the catamaran and the splashing, the ocean's surface now looked like a beautiful undulating colored mosaic with a sparkling silver background.

I noticed all the number one paddles in the canoes had raised their hands to indicate we should wait before throwing our leis to join the others already in the water.

I looked to the beach where everyone who had remained threw their flowers into the ocean. These made a colorful blanket near the shore. In time, they would be carried out with the tide.

Finally, the surfers stopped splashing and began to head back towards land. The number one paddles in the canoes signaled for us to start forward. We moved closer to the center where we stopped and removed our leis. Together we threw them to join the others.

As I tossed mine, I glanced toward the catamaran and realized Malia was watching. I nodded at her, and she nodded back. I could see the shine of tears upon her cheeks.

I hoped the ceremony had brought some closure to the family. I knew it had for me.

Finally, the *kahuna* began the familiar chant with which we ended each of our paddles. Somehow, repeating the familiar words seemed a fitting ending.

The catamaran slowly started its return trip to the harbor, and the canoes began the paddle back to shore. Since we were the farthest out, we waited until the others were near shore to start. I was happy to have a few extra seconds to appreciate the beauty of the day and the mixture of colors on the water.

Just as we began moving, I heard a motor approaching from behind us at quite a clip. We turned to look and saw a big white boat roar through the flowers and ashes we'd just placed on the water.

I thought the driver looked a bit like Jamie, and there was someone else aboard as well.

After racing through the center of what had been our circle, the boat zoomed off again. I heard gasps and muttered swearing from my team. I hoped the family on the catamaran had missed the performance. For me, it was the desecration of a holy place and put a damper on the ceremony.

Fortunately, most of the surfers were already onshore and didn't appear to have seen. Only our canoe and one other were close enough to know where the boat had gone. I looked over at the other paddlers. One caught my eye and shook his head sadly.

We headed again for shore, and I started a mental list of the people I wanted to talk to, starting with a certain lovely older couple.

Chapter 20: Slade

After our team pulled the outrigger onto the beach and stored the paddles in the club's equipment box, I drove Doc to pick up his SUV and parked my vehicle in the spot he'd occupied. I grabbed my camera from the glove box and slid it into the pocket of my trunks. Then Doc drove me back and everyone climbed into his larger vehicle for the short drive to Hale'iwa Beach Park for the luau. I slid into the rear seat between Keola and Barbara so Naomi could sit in front. Terry climbed through the rear door and pulled it shut behind him. He squatted in back with his arms around his knees and said nothing. He hadn't uttered a word since the explanation for his last-minute arrival. I leaned over the backseat.

"You're sure quiet, Terry. Feel all right?"

"Guess I'm just tired," he said. "All the planning for today plus playing nursemaid to guests on the yacht has really been a drag. I'll be glad when it's over."

"Lots of people visiting?"

I know no one was aboard this morning. What's Terry hiding?

"Actually only one," he replied. "But she can be demanding."

"The blonde?" I saw Terry's eyes widen.

"You've seen her?"

"No, just heard about her someplace. Who is she?"

"She's a Fowler family friend, over for a visit. That's all."

Terry didn't sound convincing. But I got no more information from him as we'd arrived at the luau. He quickly opened the rear door and disappeared into the crowd.

A large section of the park had been cordoned off for the event. As I arrived with Doc and Naomi, I noticed the group of Hawaiians I'd encountered earlier, working as security. Each member wore the distinctive black trunks and a dark tee shirt. Their leader, Ekana—at least I think that's what Keola had called him—waved me through with the others. The paparazzi and press were kept outside.

A long serving table had been set up in one of the covered picnic areas, and I saw all sorts of Hawaiian delicacies. The smells of pit-roasted Kalua pig and teriyaki chicken mingled with the natural plumeria and *pohuihui,* or beach morning glory, of the park.

Senator Fowler and Keilani greeted guests at the south end, he in a dark blue printed Hawaiian shirt and she in matching fitted *holoku*. That's a long dress with a short train based on a Victorian-era wedding gown. Gerry loves the style and finally bought one for herself a few months before, to wear to a friend's wedding.

Slade and Nicki Weaver stood nearby with Malia and

Mano, who I now realized were Philip's grandparents. Slade had his arm around Nicki as he had on the catamaran.

Seated at a table away from the others, looking out of place in their dark business suits, were the California Fowlers, the older Mrs. Fowler in high heels. *Must be tough walking on the beach in those.* Terry had immediately headed in their direction. I turned to greet Slade, Nicki, and the grandparents.

"Mr. Jones," Malia said as I approached, "I saw you at the paddle-out. It was nice of you to honor our grandson that way."

I knew she'd seen me and was aware that I'd recognized her. "You didn't tell me you were related to Philip."

"At first, I wanted to find out more about this so-called friend of Nicki's who mysteriously turned up on her front porch. After she told us what you were doing here, Mano and I thought you'd figure it out on your own." Malia and Mano smiled at each other as he placed an arm around his wife's shoulders.

"I assumed you were related to Nicki," I said.

"She's like the granddaughter we never had," Malia replied, taking Nicki's hand. There was sadness in her voice. *She must be realizing with Philip's death, her hope of having Nicki as a real granddaughter died as well.*

"I need to see you alone," Slade said in a low voice. "I talked to Nicki and my mom last night. They say you can be trusted."

"I can," I replied.

"I'm a little busy right now." He indicated the line of arriving people. "I'll find you later."

"Good."

Our discussion was interrupted as several newcomers approached. I moved on and turned to study the crowd. A small group, two guitars and several ukuleles, played soft Hawaiian music near a cluster of palms. People milled about, many carrying plates piled high with food. I filled one for myself from the buffet and found a quiet bench to observe the activity.

Terry was busy taking food, drinks, and whatever to the California Fowlers' table. He didn't look happy.

No sign of the blonde either.

I saw Tommy and waved. He came over carrying his own plate.

"Like the pig?" he asked as he sat next to me.

"Sure do," I answered.

"Good, 'cause Toshi and I were up early this morning starting the *imu.*"

"Before you went fishing?"

"Yeah, man. Was one big pig. We knew the crowd would be huge. Takes a lot to feed this many people." He gestured toward the hundreds of folks who continued to arrive. "But I caught some of the fish. They on the table over there. Grilled 'em all, too."

"I'll have to try some. Everything is delicious," I said, all thoughts of diet forgotten for this one day.

Toshi ambled over to us. "You gonna reopen or what?"

"Guess so. Lots of people here. Maybe some want surfing

stuff." Tommy took a last big bite and wiped the back of his hand over his mouth. "See you later, man," he called to me, and then they were gone.

I took my time finishing my heaping plate. I hadn't lied. Everything was wonderful. As I ate I enjoyed the music, always keeping one eye on the crowd.

Since long before I came to the islands, I've been fond of the soft guitar and harmonies of Hawaiian music. As a little kid, I remember my mother listening to Harry Owens and the Royal Hawaiians on the radio. She would dance around the room, pretending she was doing the hula. I often wondered if she had also seen the Gauguin paintings which had triggered my lifelong desire to live in the islands. And I wondered if I was living out her dream as well as mine.

Lovey, maybe I'm here for both of us.

I could almost feel her smile.

A couple of guys joined the musicians to sing. I felt like nodding off, and I might have done just that for a moment.

"Mr. Jones?" a voice said from behind me as I woke with a start. I turned to face Slade Fowler. He wore the same Hawaiian shirt and black slacks as his father, but there the resemblance ended. His dark hair, skin, and features matched his mother's and clearly showed his Hawaiian ancestry.

"Yes?" I replied as he glanced around.

"Let's go somewhere less crowded."

I dropped my empty plate into a trash bin and followed him first toward the ocean, then west along it. He finally stopped near a large palm tree on the bluff overlooking both the sea and the marina. No one was in the immediate vicinity.

He didn't make eye contact at first. "I wouldn't have talked to you, except both Mom and Nicki said I should. The local cops have had it in for my dad for years. And some of the attention's rubbed off on me. I get stopped and questioned all the time. But I'm not saying anything to them."

"I'm working with the police, you know," I said.

"Yeah, but you were hired and paid for by Dad. That makes a difference. He thinks you can do the job. Can you?" He looked directly at me. "I intend to find my brother's killer, no matter what it takes."

"Better leave the investigation to the professionals. There's already been one murder. And most murderers know they have little to lose by adding another victim."

"But I feel responsible! Nicki says Flip left to look for me the night he disappeared. She thinks he was headed for the Liquid Excitement shop because he thought I might have gone there. Nicki suspects they had something to do with his murder. But I think it was the North Shore developers. If it was, then it's really all my fault!" He turned and slammed his fist hard against the tree trunk.

I stood silently, letting Slade vent his rage. I was surprised when he suddenly began to sob, shoulders slumped, forehead pressed against the rough surface. I waited until his grief slowed to soft gulps. Finally, he raised his head and turned to look at me, his eyes red-rimmed.

"Where were you the night your brother disappeared?" I asked quietly and as gently as I could.

He looked slightly ashamed.

"Partying over in Kailua."

"Can anyone verify that?"

He shook his head. "Nah. I didn't really know anybody in the couple of places I stopped. I didn't even drink much. After a while, I just parked and took a long walk on the beach."

"And no one saw you?"

Again he shook his head. "I had some decisions to make."

"About what?"

He hesitated, then began. "About nine months ago, I was approached by one of the big developers. They offered me money, a lot of money, if I could persuade Dad to vote their way. I took it at first. It made the down payment on my car, and I bought some clothes and a bunch of other things. But when Dad found out, he was furious. He said if the news hit the press, it would compromise his position in the senate and lose him the next election for sure. He also said the humiliation would be hardest on Mom and insisted I cut off all contact immediately."

"Did you?"

"I tried, but they said we had a deal and if I couldn't deliver, they wanted their money back. Even made some veiled threats. Nothing I could prove, of course. So, when Flip was killed…" His voice choked.

"I saw you leaving Shari, Taylor, and Rugh yesterday. What was that about?" I asked quietly.

"You did?" Slade looked surprised. Then he sighed. "I'd had it. I accused them of killing Flip. They denied it. Said I'd better not spread rumors like that or they'd sue me for slander. Mark Taylor and I had a major shouting match. I still think they had something to do with my brother's murder. I just can't prove it. That's why I need your help."

"What do you want me to do?"

"Talk to the local cops. Have them put a tail on Mark. He's the ringleader. Cops need to follow him like they do me. I'm sure something will turn up."

"And what do you intend to do?"

"Me? I had a long talk with Dad late last night. I plan on repaying all the money I got from those bastards. Every cent. I already sold my car this morning to the Middle Eastern guy who wanted it before I got it. Paid me more than I bought it for, so I'm off the hook. Got myself an older model I can afford. If the cops won't do it, I plan on tailing Mark Taylor myself."

"Be careful. Like I said, it's better to leave the investigating to the police."

"Not if you don't trust them." He looked defiant. "And I don't. Besides, I'm afraid Nicki might be in danger."

"Why do you say that?"

"I've seen a suspicious looking car down the block from her house for a while. I don't like it. I'm afraid they're going to do something to her next."

I already knew that the black car belonged to the police, but I didn't tell Slade. *So, he's been watching out for her. Or is it just that he's been at his grandparents?*

"I noticed how protective of Nicki you've been today," I

said, hoping to find out more about their relationship. She and his mother had both defended him, and I hoped they were right.

He glanced away and seemed a bit embarrassed. The hot-head was gone for the moment. "Nicki was the best thing in my brother's life," he said softly.

He looked up and seemed to feel more explanation was necessary. "Oh, he deserved her. And she truly loved him. She was hurt when he decided to go to grad school in California. She expected they'd get married as soon as he graduated, and she had a right to want that. But Flip always thought about the future. He told me he was planning on making a good living for both of them."

"How did you see it?"

He laughed, but without any trace of humor. "If I'd been in his shoes, I'd have married her as soon as she'd have me and plan later. But that wasn't my little bro. He was methodical and logical—two things I guess I'll never be."

"Nicki seems genuinely fond of you."

"I'm fond of her, too. In fact, if I'd met her first..." He seemed to think he'd said too much and stopped. "But I didn't. Flip did, and I was happy for both of them."

"Weren't you ever jealous of all the attention your brother got? After all, he was a good student, star athlete, had lots of friends..."

"Heck, no," he answered quickly. "I was always proud of the kid. Even as a little guy, he was a standout. *Tutu-kane*...uh...our grandfather taught both of us to surf. I was okay, but Flip was great. He'd stick with something as long as it took to master it. I guess I'm just lazy. If it doesn't come easily, I give up." He made eye contact. "He deserved all the fame. I never wanted it."

I guess I looked skeptical.

"Look, Mr. Jones, Flip was my best friend. Everybody loved him. I was no exception. He was just a really loveable guy. I never envied any of the good things that came to him. Well, maybe Nicki, but I wasn't going to do anything about that. Maybe some people thought we were rivals or something, but that just wasn't true."

Nicki had told me the same thing. So had Keilani, in a way. Now that I was hearing it from Slade, I figured maybe there was some truth there. Or else all of them protested too much. But Slade seemed sincere, and so had Nicki.

"Slade, I'll make you the same promise I made to your mother. I'll do my very best to find your brother's killer."

"That's all I ask," he replied.

He held out his hand and I shook it. I meant what I'd said. I'd stay until the case was resolved. At least that was my intention at that moment.

But I wondered at his sudden changes in mood. *Could his rage have somehow been triggered by his brother? Or is he really as shaken as he seems?*

Chapter 21: Family Drama

I slowly followed Slade back to the luau. My bum leg was starting to ache from the walk and the paddle.

As I arrived, I looked for a place to sit. Naomi, as if reading my thoughts, motioned me to a picnic table with Doc and her. They moved closer together, and I slipped in on the end, grateful for the bench.

"Thanks," I said.

"We saved a place for you," Naomi answered.

I rubbed my leg. "I'm glad. I needed it."

The late afternoon sun was inching slowly toward the horizon. Since it was summer, it would remain light until after seven. A gentle breeze moved the palm fronds overhead.

I looked around to take note of what was happening. After all, I was still working, and I'd promised I'd stick around to help find the killer—or killers.

Families had spread blankets on the ground and settled in. People filled nearly every empty place on the benches. Groups I recognized as the surfers who'd taken part in the ceremony sat clumped together, their surfboards scattered about behind them like so many abandoned children's toys.

Musicians and singers exchanged places from time to time, and the music continued uninterrupted.

I spotted several undercover cops trying to be inconspicuous at the back of the crowd. But I can ID a surveillance team. Masa, however, was not among them.

I glanced at the senator's parents' table and noticed a blonde matching Tommy's description. She looked like a younger version of the elder Mrs. Fowler. Blonde hair, navy dress with matching jacket, and it appeared she was wearing hose with her heels. Gerry threw hers away as soon as we arrived. I wondered when the young gal had shown up since there were already several beers in front of her. The California Fowlers had accumulated even more. They looked like wine drinkers to me, but I hadn't seen any of that around.

Terry stopped by our table. "Anyone for a refill?" he asked, pointing to the six-pack he held.

"Thanks but I'm sticking to diet soda." I still felt as though I was on duty and wanted my faculties intact. I started to stand up.

Terry gestured me back down. "I'll bring one by on my next run." He looked at Naomi.

"We're fine." She pointed at the cans in front of her and Doc.

I watched Terry return to the California table. He parked the entire six-pack in front of the parents and the blonde. I suspected it might not last long at the rate they were going.

"When will this shindig be over?" I asked.

Naomi laughed. "Not until sometime tomorrow morning. As long as the beer and the food hold out, the people will stay."

"The family, too?"

"Oh, yes," she answered. "The best parts are yet to come. It would be rude for them to leave before the performers begin and everyone has had a chance to 'talk story'."

"And that could take all night," Doc added.

Just then a group with drums and gourds arrived and began to set up next to the guitar and uke players. I recognized the earmarks of a hula school. A local one from Kihei entertains at the authors' conference where I volunteer every Labor Day Weekend.

I was surprised and delighted to see that the dancers this time would be the *keki*, the little ones. Gerry says I'm terrible when it comes to guessing ages, particularly those of children. They all look like babies to me. But I would have sworn some of these tots couldn't have been more than two or three. The oldest seemed to be pre-adolescent.

A lady with white hair and wearing a pink-print *muumuu* tried to corral them. It was a bit like the old cliché of trying to herd cats. But she finally succeeded in getting them lined up. The drums started. Then the leader began to chant a *mele* which the tiny dancers echoed.

I had to laugh at the smallest one. She was very serious and performed each move precisely and with concentration. The one who looked next youngest, on the other hand, swayed a little and grinned at the audience.

Of course, they got a huge round of applause.

"Aren't they adorable?" Naomi whispered.

I nodded. Watching the performance took me back to when our kids were small.

Our daughter, Glenda, decided she wanted to be a ballerina when she was about three. She started lessons at around four, after nagging her mother and me for months. She was a flower for her first performance, as I recall. Just like these tykes, she made up for lack of skill with sheer cuteness. Of course, her doting dad thought she was the best one of all and treated the whole family to ice cream to celebrate her triumphant debut.

I was surprised when she continued her lessons through her first year of high school. By then, she'd appeared in the chorus of *The Nutcracker* about a dozen times. She was even on point. But she finally realized just how much hard work and pain it would require to become really good and knew she wasn't willing to suffer that much. Instead, she took up tennis and never looked back. I think Gerry still has Glenda's first tiny pink ballet slippers packed away somewhere.

Martin, our son, studied the clarinet for a short while. He even played in one recital. I must admit, I was very relieved when he decided to give it up to play baseball. The clarinet, in his unskilled hands, sounded like the cry of a sick calf. Gerry and I weren't sure how much more our ears could take, but we wanted to encourage his interest in music. Well, Gerry did. I think even she secretly celebrated when the clarinet was packed away for the last time, although she never admitted it. When we moved to Hawaii, she donated it to a local school. I fervently hoped the parents of the next student to use it had good earplugs.

The little kids performed another number, and then they were joined by lovely teenagers. As they moved together to the beat, I marveled, as I always do, at how beautiful the dance is.

Next, the older woman escorted the small fry away. Then the girls performed "Sweet Lelani" while a young man with a beautiful voice played guitar and sang.

I remembered that Harry Owens composed the song, and I wished Lovey were with me to hear it. Hilo Hattie had sung it on the radio. Whenever I pass one of the many stores in Hawaii which bear her name, that song comes to mind.

During the dance, the black shirts set tiki torches around the perimeter of the park and lit them, bathing the whole place in a soft glow. The sky turned from pink to orange to purple. Just another gorgeous sunset in Hawaii. I pulled out my camera and snapped off a few shots of the sunset and the dancers.

After the applause died down and the girls exited, I was surprised to see the older woman return to take their place. She gestured to the audience. Several other ladies, including Malia, joined her. These were the *tutus*—the grandmas.

Gerry and I had seen other mature dancers before, and we agreed they were often more graceful than the young girls. Maybe they had practiced longer, or perhaps it was the way their *muumuus* moved to the music. These gals were good.

I grabbed my camera and took a couple of photos of Malia and the ladies.

They performed two numbers. Then the hula school began to pack their equipment.

I saw Malia headed my way and stood to greet her.

"I hope I'll get a copy of those pictures," she said. "Nicki has email."

"I'll get her address before I leave."

We both glanced over to where the lady in question stood. Slade remained next to her as he had all day.

"I've noticed how attentive he's been today," I observed, wondering what her reaction would be.

"Yes. My grandson is a good boy. They both are…were." She paused. "My Philip had *lokomaika'i*." When I gave her a puzzled look, she explained, "English doesn't have the same word. It means kindness, generosity. But it's much more than that." She thought for a moment. "It is sharing kindness from within, from a place in your soul."

I nodded my understanding.

"The *ali'i* understood that real wealth comes not from possessions but in the ability to give generously of what you possess. Philip understood this and showed his on the outside. Slade keeps his more inside, but it is there."

She looked over at the two young people. Slade had taken Nicki's hand.

"Nicki has *lokomaika'i,* too."

I nodded again. I knew she didn't expect anything more.

She kissed my cheek and then returned to Mano's side.

I knew I'd always have a special place in my heart for this precious couple and their family.

During the hula, Terry had dropped off a diet soda for me and taken another six-pack to the Fowler table. It didn't last long.

The music started again, at first softly. However, as the evening progressed, it got louder and more raucous. But not loud enough to drown out what happened next.

I watched as the senator left Keilani's side and crossed the picnic area to approach his parents' table. His mother leaned over and whispered something to the blonde, who stood and intercepted the senator. She looped one arm possessively through his and kissed him on the cheek. It seemed a bit too long.

Senator Fowler removed her arm and tried to brush past her. He started to say something to his parents, but the blonde shouted, "You can't get rid of me that easily." Her voice carried on the breeze. "Why don't you admit you made a mistake and leave her? You know I'm higher class and would make a much more appropriate wife. Besides, I'm better in bed."

The senator reached for her arm and said something I couldn't hear. But this time, she brushed his hand away.

Out of the corner of my eye, I spotted Terry moving through the crowd, but he wasn't close enough to do anything.

To my surprise, the older Mrs. Fowler said in a voice too loud and slightly slurred, "You know she's right. We chose her for you years ago."

"Now, dear..." Her husband attempted to stop her tirade.

Mom was on her feet now. "You moved away without our permission. Then you married a nobody—a nothing. And even worse, a foreign nobody." She emphasized the word 'foreign.'

I wondered if anyone ever told her that Hawaiians are as American as she is. But I figured she wouldn't listen anyway.

I watched the same look appear on Senator Fowler's face that I'd seen on his son's a couple of hours earlier. With barely controlled rage, he spoke. "Mother, I left because you never listened to me. You still don't. You expected me to do your bidding without protest. But it's my life. And the choices were mine to make. As for you, Brooke." He turned to face the blonde. "I made a mistake once. But it's not one I intend to make again. It's over."

He turned and strode away.

Good for you, Senator, I thought.

The blonde looked as though the man had hit her, and I was afraid Mrs. Fowler was going to faint. Terry arrived in time to ease her back onto the bench. Her husband sat motionless.

Brooke started to follow the senator, but Terry got to her quickly. He said something I couldn't make out, but I heard her response.

"I don't want to." She sounded like a petulant child. Gone was the bravado of just a moment before.

"Come on, now," he said and led her away. She went quietly. The senior Fowlers followed.

"What was that all about?" I asked Naomi.

She sighed. "Old news. A few years ago, Keilani and Tom were going through a rough patch, just like every couple."

I knew what she meant. As much as I love Gerry, we've had a few of those over the years.

"Then Brooke showed up, and Tom gave her a job in his office. It became something more than just a job, if you know what I mean."

I nodded.

"It didn't last long before Tom broke it off and sent her back to California. But Keilani found out. It took a couple of years of serious counseling for them to put the pieces back together again. I was surprised to see Brooke here today."

"She's been staying on the yacht this week," Doc said quietly.

Naomi spun to face him. "And you didn't tell me? It's my yacht, after all."

Doc looked sheepish. "I figured it was better to have her here where Terry could keep an eye on her, than in Honolulu."

"But why didn't the two of you ask me about it? Or at least tell me?"

"Because we knew what your reaction would be."

"Why did she come at all?"

"Terry said she arrived with the senator's parents and they insisted she stay. You know his mother. She doesn't give up easily."

Naomi laughed, but without humor. "Now there's an understatement. She doesn't give up at all. Her attempts to manipulate her son have been going on for years."

"I'm glad he finally told her off. I'll bet Terry is, too. He said he's tired of babysitting the spoiled brat."

During their conversation, they'd forgotten about me.

Naomi seemed to remember I was there and faced me again. "Not many people know about all this. Well, at least they didn't until now." She glanced in Keilani's direction. "I hope she's okay." She started to rise, but Doc stopped her.

"Better wait until she asks," he said.

"I guess you're right." She sat again.

We watched as the senator, phone to his ear, escorted his wife from the park. Their limousine pulled up, and George hopped out to open the door.

Doc put an arm around Naomi. "I think it's time we left, too. Want a ride back to your car, Agapé?"

It was the best offer I'd had all day.

Chapter 22: Aftermath

I was suddenly awakened in the pre-dawn hours.

"Damned alarm," I muttered as I searched the unfamiliar night table in the darkened room. It took a few seconds before I realized the sound was coming from the hotel phone. Blinking hard to squeeze the sleep from my eyes, I answered.

"Agapé Jones here."

"Mister Jones, this is Detective Watanabe. We need to talk. How soon can you meet me at the Café Hale'iwa?"

I glanced at the bedside clock and read four forty-five. *Must be really important for Masa to call this early.*

"Give me forty minutes. I just woke from a sound sleep."

"Very well. I'll see you then." Masa hung up.

I hurried through my PT routine to get the bum leg moving. It was a little stiff after all the activity the day before. Then I quickly showered, shaved, dressed, and headed up Kam Highway toward the café. As I traveled, I recalled the events of the previous night.

* * * *

We'd watched the senator's limo drive off.

"Better find the rest of the family," Naomi insisted as we rose from the picnic table. "It's not polite to just leave without saying good night."

"Well, would you look at that?" Doc said, pointing across the park in the direction of the marina.

In the moonlight, I could just make out the silhouettes of the Fowler grandparents, the blonde, and Terry as they crested a far sand dune. I had to smile. Terry was escorting, perhaps 'herding' was a better word, the other three across the rugged marina shortcut trail rather than following the park's longer, but paved and lighted path.

"Must be payback time," Doc mused. "That's a tough trail even in daylight. Bet Terry's secretly enjoying watching two tipsy women struggle across the sand in high heels."

Naomi, Doc, and I located Slade, Nicki, Malia, and Mano to thank them and say goodbye. We left them still mixing with the guests.

"Looks like Hawaiian 'talk story' will continue late tonight," Naomi whispered.

As we exited the park, Ekana, with a stern, intimidating expression and arms crossed over his black tee shirt, stepped aside to let us through. I looked back as we reached Doc's SUV, and he was still watching. He raised one hand in the *shaka* sign. But it reminded me more of a military salute than a friendly gesture. His expression never changed.

Passing the marina, I saw lights and activity on the yacht. Naomi noticed too. She scowled but said nothing. Doc dropped me off at my car.

"Remember, we practice again day after tomorrow. Hope you can make it," Doc said.

"I'll let you know."

As I pulled out into traffic, I noticed it was pretty heavy and figured some of the crowd from the luau were heading home. *Better be extra cautious, Jones*, I said to myself. *There was a lot of drinking going on tonight.*

I was especially glad I'd stuck to diet coke when a pickup full of kids approached from behind at high speed. The road wasn't really wide enough for passing, and we were nearing the curve at the far side of Waimea Bay.

I suddenly remembered that this was where Naomi's first husband had been killed.

I slowed, hoping the driver would decrease his speed as well. But the guy skidded around me, nearly leaving the road, straightened out a bit, then careened around the bend.

I waited for the sound of a crash and was relieved when all that reached my ears was silence.

By the time I made the turn, they had disappeared.

"I hope they make it home in one piece," I said aloud.

I parked in the lot at the hotel and removed my wet swimsuit and towel from the trunk. They'd been enclosed in the heat all day, and both were pretty ripe. I dropped the trunks in the sink in the kitchenette and took the towel out to the lanai. I figured if I draped it over one of the chairs, it would be dry by morning. And I hoped the breeze would remove some of the stale smell.

Then I washed out the suit with soap, rinsed it well, and hung it over the shower rod.

It was late, and I didn't want to wake Gerry, but I noticed the light on the phone. She had left three messages, the last one only a few minutes before.

"Agapé, please call me, even if it's late. I can't sleep."

On our wedding night, I'd told my bride about my grandparents. They were married for nearly seventy years when my grandfather died.

Shortly afterward, Granny told me, "I miss him the most at night. For all those years, no matter what was happening, we never went to sleep without kissing and telling each other, 'I love you.' I miss that kiss and those words. I just can't get to sleep."

She died a few months later. Her death certificate said 'heart failure,' but I always felt she just wanted to be with Gramps.

I loved that story, and we decided to make it a part of our nightly routine. We've seldom missed in over forty years.

After my long, emotional day, I really needed to hear her voice.

She answered on the first ring. "I'm so glad you called. I've been watching the whole funeral on TV all afternoon. I couldn't help but relate to that poor woman and imagine how awful it must be to lose a child. What if it were Martin or Glenda?"

"I'm just glad they're both safe at home. It was hard for the whole family. I hope you'll get to meet them sometime.

They're really great people. That's what makes the situation even more tragic."

"I think I saw you in one of the canoes. Were you in the third spot?"

"Yep. Just like at home."

"I thought so. You were near the big boat with the family."

"Yes."

"Where have you been since then? I thought the whole thing ended after they threw the flowers in the water."

I chuckled. "That was just the second ending. The first was at the church in Honolulu. After we paddled back in, there was a big luau with lots of food and entertainment. Some little girls danced. It reminded me of some of Glenda's performances. I wished you could have seen them."

"I've missed being with you. Maggie and Chuck asked me to go to dinner again, but it wasn't the same without you."

"I wish you could get away for a couple of days and come for a visit."

"So do I, but I still have my class to consider. I can't abandon the kids, especially since they're really enthusiastic. It's one of the things I love about these special summer programs. Only the ones who are really interested attend."

"Glad to hear it's going well and that Chuck and Maggie are there."

"But I still wish you here beside me. The bed is awfully big."

"Miss you, sweetheart. I love you."

"Love you, too," she answered.

There was a long pause while each of us waited for the other to hang up. Finally, I heard a click on the other end of the line.

I turned on the TV and scenes from the day's activities appeared. I watched the crowd coming out of the church. Then there were shots of the caravan arriving at the marina, the boat leaving, and the paddle-out. I spotted our canoe and watched clips of the events as they appeared from the air. Replaying them made me sad again, so I clicked the set off.

While it was still fresh in my memory, I jotted a few notes.

I suddenly realized how exhausted—physically and emotionally—I was. So I turned off the lights and dropped off.

* * * *

It was still before sunrise when I arrived at the Café Hale'iwa. Fortunately, I'd been there the day before and was able to find the place easily. Masa waited at one of the outdoor tables under a blue umbrella at the side of the restaurant.

"The place doesn't open for breakfast till seven. I picked up an extra coffee on my way over," he said, pointing to a foam cup on the table. "I remembered you take cream and sugar."

I sat down across from him and took a sip. It tasted like the sludge they make in every police station. But it was hot.

"Okay, what's up?"

"I've been working several big cases recently. We're not

only investigating Philip's murder, but also several vandalism and harassment complaints involving North Shore development. They're increasing, and the situation could flare up at any time.

"Then, there's a major shark-poaching ring working this side of the island. We've been able to isolate the poachers to somewhere in the Waialua district, but we don't have any direct leads. They appear to be well-organized. Somehow, they're able to get their goods to cargo vessels bound for China. We just don't know how."

Masa paused and took a drink of his coffee, then looked directly at me.

"I saw you at the luau yesterday and on the bluff talking to Slade. I was stuck down at the marina. You seem to have gained entry into the local community. My officers are too well known and mistrusted by the locals. We need someone on the inside. Someone they feel is not out to get them. Someone like you."

I leaned forward and took another sip. "Listen, I came here to investigate the murder of a young man. My first priority is just that. I don't intend to get involved in other police work."

"We think all these activities might be related."

I set my cup down, sat back, and considered Masa's statement. I was still reluctant but finally I asked, "What do you want me to do?"

"Just continue with your investigation and keep your eyes and ears open. If anything shows up, alert me immediately.

You have my cell number." I confirmed the number and added it to my speed dial. I looked up at him.

"Okay, I'll let you know if I see anything. But Philip is my priority."

"I understand."

He glanced around. "I must be going. It'll be light soon and people will be arriving. We shouldn't be seen together." He headed for his unmarked cruiser.

I looked down at Masa's empty cup. "Hey," I called after him. "I thought the next time we met I was supposed to pick up the tab."

He turned back and smiled. "You just did."

Glancing at my watch, I realized I still had more than an hour before the café opened. I could go back to the car, but at six in the morning, where would I go? Who would I see?

Might as well stay here and enjoy the sunrise.

I opened my notebook, took another swig of my cooling brew, and scribbled a new note.

Vandalism, shark poaching, murder – Possible connection?

I've heard about the shark finning operation on the news. And I've been told plenty about the North Shore situation. Masa suspects Philip's murder may be linked to a larger plot. My investigation hasn't turned up any credible suspects. No one seems to have had a clear motive or even the inclination to want him dead. Everyone liked him, so I must be missing something. But what?

I could almost hear Lovey's voice.

'Son, you've hit blind alleys and dead ends before. When you run into a stone wall, what do you do?'

I take a step back and try another direction.

'Right, but what direction?'

Well, if Masa's right, I need to widen my net. Time to look at the facts again.

'I knew you'd figure it out, honey, you always do.' Her voice in my head faded into memory.

I really miss that lady. But I'm grateful for all the years of her encouragement.

I turned the notebook to the beginning page, and started down the list of notes.

Dead surfer floating off Maui.
Apparent stab wound to chest.
Identified as Philip Fowler—disappeared from Oahu three days earlier.

He couldn't have drifted that far. He had to have been transported. That suggests a ship or boat. There are plenty in Hale'iwa Harbor, including a yacht capable of reaching Maui in several hours.

I flipped a few pages.

Toxicology report: polystyrene in victim's mouth and ears

I looked at the coffee cup before me.

They make foam cups and packing materials from polystyrene.

Could the body have been packed away in the stuff until we found him? But how? And where would polystyrene dust fine enough come from?

I looked through my notes from Nicki.

He was going to the Liquid Excitement factory looking for Slade the night he disappeared.

But Jake said Slade hadn't been there in a while. They use foam for surfboards.

I checked the notes I made after talking to Wacko. *He said Malcolm's board is made from polyethylene. Polyethylene not polystyrene. It's a different material. Still, they pack boards for shipment overseas, so maybe that's involved somehow.*

Finally, I turned back to my notes from Nicki.

Philip overheard Bob Hillman on the phone saying something about needing to teach Slade a lesson.

Could the murder have anything to do with Slade reneging on his deal with the North Shore developers? Are they connected to Liquid Excitement?

'So, son,' Lovey's voice boomed into my thoughts. *'Looks like your pieces may fit together. What do you do now?'*

"Well," I said aloud, even though there was no one nearby, "I need to see if there's any connection between the North Shore developers and the surfboard factory."

Maybe Tommy can tell me. And it's time I had a little face-to-face talk with Bob Hillman. Probably won't learn much, but it's worth a try. And what was the name of the developer? Mark Taylor, that's it. Better talk to him too.

'Good, son. But first have some breakfast. You'll need your strength and it looks like the Café is about to open.'

Chapter 23: The Abduction

I was the morning's first guest at the café.

"Sit anywhere you like," the waitress said as she opened the door. She was a young girl who looked to be in her early twenties with her sun-streaked blonde hair pulled back in a long ponytail, wearing a short Hawaiian-print dress covered by a light blue apron.

As I entered, she pulled upside-down chairs from atop the tables and returned them to their proper positions.

"Grab a menu." She pointed in the general direction of the serving counter, still busy readying the place for the morning crowd.

I took a seat near the back wall facing the front door, a habit of my NYPD days. From here, I could observe the entire room and see anyone approaching.

"Cook's not in yet. I can take your order, but it'll probably be a few minutes before you get it."

"That's all right. Is there any coffee?" I thought I smelled it brewing.

"It should be ready in just a sec." She smiled. "I can't get my eyes open without it."

"Neither can I. Can you bring some when it's done?"

"Sure." She disappeared into the kitchen. I heard a door bang and the sound of voices.

In a couple of minutes, she was back.

"Kona blend," she said, placing a steaming cup in front of me. It smelled heavenly. Then she pulled the order pad and pen from her apron pocket. "Cook just got here. What ya want?"

"I'd like two eggs, over easy, bacon crisp, and wheat toast."

"That's all? You can get that stuff anyplace. This is Hawaii. I like the *Off the Wall* omelet or the Hawaiian sweet bread French toast, but you can't go wrong with anything on the menu."

I shook my head. "My wife would shoot me if I ordered either of those. I'd hear about the fat and sugar for weeks." I added sugar and cream to my coffee. It smelled better than my earlier cup, and I couldn't wait for a taste. It seemed like hours since my visit with Masa.

"Well, we got fresh papaya this morning."

"Okay, add half a papaya."

She smiled brightly. "Comin' right up."

Several other people came in. The waitress seemed to know most of them and greeted them by name.

I'd just finished my breakfast when I saw Jake enter.

I heard the waitress say from behind me, "Hi, Jake."

"I'll take my usual, Sally," he called back.

I saw her nod, then head toward the kitchen.

I waved to him and pointed to the chair across from me. He came over and sat down.

"So you took my advice, huh, Mr. Jones? Like I said, they serve the best breakfast in town."

"How's my grandson's board coming?" I inquired to make small talk.

"It should be on schedule. But I'm ticked off this morning. I haven't seen Jamie or Cho since before the paddle-out yesterday, and Wacko said he'd come in early today. I drove past the factory on my way here, and it was still dark inside. Bet they're off on that boat of Jamie's again. It seems to happen a lot lately."

The waitress arrived with Jake's steak, two eggs, and a large glass of orange juice. She refilled my coffee.

"I meet Toshi here for breakfast every Thursday morning. He does my bookkeeping."

"Toshi? I thought he helped Tommy run the surfboard shop."

"He does. But he's also an accountant. I'm no good at numbers. Neither is Tommy. Toshi manages all that stuff so we can concentrate on our businesses."

That was a surprise. Although, come to think of it, Toshi, with his pidgin English and quiet personality, seemed better suited for number crunching than sales.

Jake continued, "We go over the receipts, check sales, inventory, everything. He should be here any time now."

"Does Tommy come, too?

Jake laughed. "Tommy never misses the chance for a free meal. Since I pick up the tab, he's usually here. Don't get me wrong. Tommy's a super guy. Give you the shirt off his back. But where food is concerned..." He shook his head slowly, leaving the rest unsaid.

"Good," I replied. "I need to talk to him."

As I drained my cup, Tommy and Toshi arrived and joined our table.

"Agapé, I seem to run into you everywhere. Don't you ever go home?" Tommy said in greeting.

"Not till I finish what I came for."

Tommy nodded but said nothing.

The waitress immediately arrived with coffee for Tommy and hot tea for Toshi.

"Same as always?" she asked.

"Yes, Sally, the regular," Tommy answered for both of them.

She glanced at Toshi, who nodded in agreement.

I excused myself for a trip to the restroom. Two cups of coffee is about my limit in the morning, and I'd already had three.

When I returned, the guys were huddled over Toshi's computer printout. To my surprise, in front of Tommy were a half a papaya and a side of toast, while stick-thin Toshi had a double order of banana pancakes, three eggs, bacon, and hash browns.

Sure can't predict a person's appetite by his size.

I motioned to Tommy and pointed to another table, but he held up his hand.

"Sit down, Agapé," he said. "This won't take long."

As I sat, Sally refilled my cup.

Toshi pointed to some numbers and said, "Jake, production way down. Plenty of orders, and your custom boards holding their own. But stock board count falling behind. Cash flow is okay. You make profit on shipping, and Japanese pay plenty for your name."

Jake set his fork down. "I'm upset with Wacko. He used to turn out fifty machine-shaped boards a day. Now he's not making half that. I'm afraid he's back on drugs again. He and Cho spend way too much time on Jamie's boat and not enough at the factory. I've been meaning to talk to them about it, but I haven't been able to catch them long enough."

Toshi frowned and turned to another paper. He moved it so Jake and Tommy could see and pointed to a number. "That bulk shipment to Japan due the end of the month." Then he pointed at another column. "That order take most of your stock. Nothing left for anyone else."

I leaned toward Tommy and whispered, "While these guys discuss business, can we talk privately?" I motioned to a just-abandoned table.

Tommy nodded, but didn't move. "In a sec."

Jake frowned and said, "I hate using the machine. It makes the same boring board each time, and I never got very fast with it. I guess I could shape a few myself, but my equipment tears up the EPS. I've looked into an abrasive drum kit for the Skill 100, but they want five hundred bucks for one. Guess now I'll just have to put out the money. Always knew I'd have to convert to EPS someday." Jake sighed and sat back in the chair. "Hope I can get the kit in time."

"What's EPS?" It was a term I hadn't heard before.

"Expanded polystyrene. It's the only core material we can get in bulk now. The polyethylene blanks with polyester resin I use for my custom boards have environmental problems. We can still buy them, and I do for my own orders. EPS is steam expanded-polystyrene, extruded into a mold under pressure."

Polystyrene. That's what I'd been looking for. Surfboard factories jumped to the front of my list of possible murder sites. I remembered the piles of foam dust around Wacko's machine. I grabbed my notebook.

"What happens to the leftover foam pieces and accumulated dust?" I asked.

"That's the best part. Cho hooked us up with this deal where we can ship the leftover EPS foam to China for recycling."

"How does that work?"

"We dump all the excess stuff into a special shipping container behind the shop. Every two weeks, a ship comes from China. They pick up the full one and leave us an empty. It's a great deal. It keeps the environmentalists and EPA off our backs. Most of the surfboard makers on this side of the island are using it. We get rid of our waste, and it doesn't cost us a dime."

I made some notes.

EPS = Polystyrene used in surfboards
Waste collected and shipped to China
Waste stored in shipping container behind Liquid Excite-ment

Now I really needed to talk to Tommy, get into the factory, and check out that shipping container.

The guys finished and Jake paid their bill. I paid mine and left a tip.

"See you guys later," Jake said. "Toshi and I are headed for his office to go over last week's receipts."

We followed them out, and Tommy and I took the end table on the lanai. It was still early, so they weren't all filled yet. Before long, the place would be packed. Besides, I liked the relative privacy.

"Tommy," I started, "you know the real reason I'm here."

"Yeah, man, to find Flip's killer. I'm with you all the way."

"What you don't know is polystyrene dust was found in Philip's nose and ears. And Nicki said he was going to the surfboard factory to look for Slade the night he disappeared. I have a hunch he might have made it. Is there a way to get into the building? Jake said no one was there when he went by."

Tommy paused, sucked on his lower lip, and then said, "Toshi has a key at the shop for emergencies, but why don't you just ask Jake to let you in?"

"The fewer people who know what I'm doing here, the better. I don't think Jake is involved, but I can't be sure."

We'd just started for the Cobalt when my cell phone rang. I answered. It was Malia.

"Mr. Jones," she said. "I'm sorry to bother you, but I'm worried. Nicki didn't come home last night and her car wasn't in her driveway when I woke up at three o'clock this morning. When you get old, you sometimes can't sleep. It was much too early for her shift. I waited for her to arrive, but she didn't. I called her cell phone, but only reached her voicemail. I thought she might be with Slade, but I just phoned him and he said he hasn't seen her since they left the luau last night. I checked with the hospital, and she hasn't reported for work either. That's not like her. Not like her at all."

I could hear the concern in her voice. "When did you last see her?"

"She and Slade were still at the park when Mano and I left."

"Slade hasn't heard from her either?" I'd seen his protectiveness the night before and was sure he'd be worried.

"No. He said she told him she was going straight home when they left the party. Slade's on his way over and should be here soon."

"If you see him, ask him to meet me at Typhoon Tommy's. Do you have his cell phone number?"

I wrote it in my notebook.

"Thank you," she said softly. Then we hung up.

For her sake, I hope I'll be able to help. We got into my car and I started it.

"Trouble?" asked Tommy.

"I hope not," I replied. *No sense in alarming him until I know more about what's going on.*

We'd just left the driveway when my cell rang again.

"Can you answer that, Tommy? I never use the phone when I'm driving."

Tommy grabbed it from the center console and answered. "Hello. No, he's driving."

"Who is it?" I asked.

"Just a minute," he said into the mouthpiece. "It's Slade Fowler."

"I need to talk to him." I pulled the car over to the side of the road.

"I understand Nicki's missing," I said into the phone.

"I'm afraid she went to the surfboard factory last night without me. I said I'd go with her, but Nicki's stubborn."

"I told both of you to leave the investigation to the professionals." I didn't mean to bark at him, but I was annoyed.

"That's what I told her, but I'm afraid she didn't listen." He sounded close to tears.

"Tommy and I are on our way to the shop right now. Meet us there."

"I will. I'm pretty close, but I'm worried."

"So am I." Then I hung up. I hoped he was using a hands-free device of some kind and that he wasn't driving too fast.

Just as we pulled into Tommy's lot, my phone rang again. I parked and picked it up.

"Jones here."

"Agapé, they have Nicki." Slade sounded short of breath as if he was running.

"Who has her?"

"Wacko, Jamie, and Cho. They're getting on Jamie's boat, but I saw them put Nicki aboard. She was tied up. Damn! They're taking off and I can't catch them."

"We'll be right there."

I restarted the car. "Tommy, we're going to need your boat."

Chapter 24: Pursuit

"What's going on?" Tommy asked as I pushed the accelerator to the floor.

I briefed him on Slade's call as the Cobalt raced up Kam Highway.

Then I remembered the bug. *Someone could have heard, but I can't worry about that now.*

Normally, it's about a five-minute drive from the shop to the marina. We didn't have five minutes. I reached the turnout just before the bridge, wishing I had a siren and lights.

No cross-traffic. I'm going for it.

The Cobalt skidded through the left turn onto Hale'iwa Road and made the entrance to the boatyard in less than three minutes.

"My Boston Whaler's at the end tie on the far side," Tommy said. "Take the road to the right along the breakwater and park all the way down."

Tommy was out of the car and running even before I

stopped. Slade spotted us and sprinted in our direction. I grabbed my phone from the front seat and hurried to catch the others as fast as my bum leg would allow. At the same time, I punched Watanabe's number on speed dial.

Damn, line's busy. Masa, get off the phone.

Tommy reached the boat first with Slade right behind him. I was moving as quickly as I could.

"Hurry up," Slade called as he untied the line from the dock.

Tommy already had the outboard motor started. I arrived and climbed in. My run and the hard landing didn't do my leg any good, but I barely noticed. *I'll feel it tomorrow, though.*

Slade cast off and jumped aboard. Tommy slammed the throttle full open and the big Mercury shot us toward the harbor entrance much faster than the posted limit.

I didn't care.

"This baby's smaller, lighter, and faster than Jamie's thirty-three-foot Grady, even with its twin Mercs," Tommy yelled. "We should be able to overtake it, but we'll need a bunch o' luck."

I hit the redial for Watanabe. This time he answered, but I could barely hear him over the sounds of the engine and the wind. I cupped my hand around the phone and crouched down close to the center console where I hoped it might be a little quieter. Even then, I had to yell and repeat myself a couple of times to be understood.

I briefed him on the situation and asked for backup.

"Please describe the craft again," Masa said in his cool, matter-of-fact manner.

I pictured him writing down the details.

"What's your current position and what direction are they headed?"

"We're still inside the harbor, and until we clear the entrance, we won't know," I answered.

"Call me as soon as you have more information," Masa directed. "Meanwhile, I'll get on it. They could be making for Kauai across the channel, so I'll alert the authorities in Lihu'e to be on the lookout. Or they may head for open sea. If the boat gets into international waters, it could get complicated."

"We'll try to make sure that doesn't happen," I answered. I heard a click and hoped that the folks Masa was calling in would mobilize and get moving quickly.

As we left the harbor, Slade yelled, "There she is, headed west along the shore past Hale'iwa surfing beach."

I called Masa back. The first time his line was busy, but on the second try I relayed the information.

Tommy had the Whaler at full throttle. The tach read sixty-two hundred. I looked at him and back at the tach.

"She'll hold together," he said as he patted the center console. "You show 'em, baby."

Slade ran to the front and leaned forward like a figurehead, his hands cupped around his eyes to reduce the glare off the water as he peered intently ahead.

I think he needs to feel as close to Nicki as possible.

"Good thing Slade's in the bow. It'll help this baby trim for top speed," Tommy said to me.

We rapidly gained on our target.

"Maybe we better back off," I told Tommy. "They could be armed, and we're not." I wanted to keep them in sight until law enforcement arrived.

"You're a cop, and you don't carry a gun?" Tommy screamed over the engine noise.

"I'm retired," I yelled back.

"Then why the hell are we trying to catch these guys?"

Just as Tommy eased back the throttle, I heard what sounded like a gunshot, and saw something hit the water ahead of the boat.

"Shit," Tommy said and slowed a little more.

Slade noticed and called back, "What do you think you're doing?"

"Trying to save your butt," Tommy answered.

The Grady made a sharp turn and accelerated out to sea.

Slade screamed as my worst fears were realized. We saw a large object tossed overboard. It sank immediately.

"Get there and hurry," Slade yelled.

Tommy had already aimed toward the location. A thinning trail of bubbles marked where the thing had disappeared. I prayed it wasn't Nicki.

We approached the spot. Without warning, Slade picked up the concrete block Tommy used for an anchor and heaved it and himself overboard.

Tommy cut the engine.

The world went quiet.

We watched the anchor rope play out, hoping the ocean under us wasn't too deep. Fortunately, the line quickly went slack.

The next twenty seconds felt like days. The sea was calm with no wind, and the only sounds were the chop slapping against the hull and the distant whine of the Grady growing faint.

Tommy and I watched bubbles rise from the dark water.

"Come on, Slade, find her," Tommy muttered from behind my shoulder. I was thinking the same thing and prayed even harder. Then the rope jerked three times.

We hauled in the line as fast as we could.

Finally, Slade's head broke the surface with an audible gasp. He grasped a body-sized burlap bag. I grabbed a handful of material and held it while Slade swam to the stern. I could already tell the sack didn't contain a body. Tommy lowered the rear ladder.

"It's not her. Go, go," Slade shouted at Tommy.

"That's the dumbest stunt I've seen yet. Gutsy, but dumb," Tommy said as he fired up the engine. "Another hundred yards out and you'd have been off the reef. The bottom out there has to be over two-hundred feet."

With the bag onboard, Slade grabbed Tommy's fishing knife from the console. Several slashes and the contents spilled out, including some large rocks.

"Shark fins," Tommy exclaimed. "Must be fifty of 'em! Illegal as hell. Bet that's why they dumped 'em. Didn't want to get caught with contraband."

"Well, it's evidence now," I replied. "Looks like more than just a kidnapping."

What the hell did Nicki get mixed up in? And does it have anything to do with Philip's death? This could be a lead in Masa's case.

We got back into the chase, but the Grady had gotten quite a head start. I could only hope Watanabe's guys would intercept, and soon.

"They're headed west," I told Masa when I reached him.

"Toward Kaena Point?" he asked.

I confirmed with Tommy and passed the information along.

"There's a Coast Guard cutter on the way. Should be there in a few..." Then the cell went quiet.

Damn, lost the signal. We're too far from shore.

"Masa says the Coast Guard's coming. We just need to follow until they get here," I told the others.

I hope they make it in time.

Slade used Tommy's binoculars to keep our target in sight and to make sure the crew didn't throw anything else—or anybody—overboard.

"We won't be able to keep this up very long," Tommy said. "I don't have enough fuel. The Grady can probably make the eighty miles to Kauai, but not us. We'll need to turn back soon or risk running out."

"You gotta keep goin', man," Slade pleaded. "It's Nicki out there."

"This baby burns over ten gallons an hour going this fast but less than seven if we cut it to below five thousand," Tommy said. "If we lighten the load, we may be able to keep it up for another half hour."

We threw the rocks and Tommy's anchor overboard, emptied the fresh water tank, and tossed anything else not critical.

"Space yourselves across the deck to keep the Whaler level and trim. We'll go faster," Tommy said as he slowed to five thousand RPM to save fuel.

Slade moved back to the bow, and I went to the stern.

Even moving a little slower, we continued to close the gap with the Grady.

Suddenly we heard two shots, and the splashes were closer to our boat this time.

"It's Cho! And he has a gun," Slade shouted. This time he could identify the shooter through the binoculars. "He just turned the gun toward Wacko. Looks like they're freaking."

"Man, that was too close," Tommy said as he slowed a little more to match their speed. "Got to keep out of pistol range."

A minute later, Slade spotted the Coast Guard cutter on an intercept course and let out a yell.

The ship quickly overtook the other vessel.

"They're boarding," Slade said, watching through the binoculars. "They're taking Cho and Wacko. Wait, I can see Nicki. She looks okay. They're putting her aboard the Coast Guard ship, too." He visibly relaxed.

"Let's follow the cutter," I said to Tommy.

"I hope they're going slow. Their base is in Kaneohe. That's on the west side of the island. We'll never make it that far."

But we were surprised when they turned. Then their loudspeaker boomed, "Follow us back to Hale'iwa Harbor."

"You bet. That we can do," Tommy said and turned the Whaler toward home.

Chapter 25: Back on Dry Land

Once the Whaler was close enough to land to get a signal, I called Masa. "You'll need to get a warrant to search the Liquid Excitement factory, especially the recycle container out back. I suspect you may find your shark fins there."

"I will take care of it. Thank you."

As we reached the harbor, the flashing lights of law enforcement cars made the place look as though Christmas had arrived early. In addition to several police vehicles (I didn't think there were that many in the area), a fire engine and a couple of ambulances stood staged and ready if needed. I'd been involved in enough evolving crime scenes in my day to recognize the setup.

Tommy quickly maneuvered his boat into its slip. Even before we stopped moving, Slade had jumped out and raced toward the spot where the Coast Guard cutter was tying up. Uniformed officers stood guard, waiting for the guys and Nicki.

"I think that's about enough excitement to last the rest of

my life," Tommy said as he shut down the motor and hopped out to fasten the line.

I climbed out as my bum leg protested. *Extra PT tomorrow and maybe a soak in the hot tub tonight.* Then it occurred to me that with any luck, I might be able to catch a plane back to Maui and my Gerry tonight if the poaching ring was somehow connected to Philip's death. Something told me it was.

Tommy slowed his pace to mine as I limped along the dock. Masa stood at the end waiting for us.

We watched as Jamie's boat arrived and pulled into his specially-equipped slip. It seemed obvious that the Coast Guard had decided not to try to remove him at sea. Here, he could just roll out. The waiting officers escorted him to the parking lot. I assumed they'd transport him in his own van since it was equipped with a ramp.

He held his head in his hands, trying to cover his face.

The press must have gotten hold of the story, because we heard voices raised and saw flashes as the wheelchair passed beyond the area cordoned off with yellow crime tape.

We reached Masa. "Good work," he said and shook my hand. Then he nodded at Tommy.

We turned to see Wacko and Cho, in handcuffs, escorted to a police car. I heard Wacko yelling, "He tried to kill me! They saw it!" He motioned to Tommy and me. "He's crazy. He made me do it."

Cho showed no reaction, and the officers paid no attention. Doors slammed, and the siren blared as the car sped off.

"Guess I'd better get back to the shop. Toshi's probably

wondering what happened to me. Have I got a story to tell!" Tommy grinned at both of us. "Barely had enough gas to get back. It was close."

"We'll see to compensation for you," Masa told him.

"Great," Tommy replied and ambled off.

"Did you search the factory?"

Masa nodded but didn't say anything.

I turned to see Slade with his arm around Nicki. Two officers escorted them toward a waiting ambulance. Since she seemed to walk easily on her own and appeared to be unharmed, she probably wouldn't require medical care. But it was a necessary precaution, and would help ease Slade's concern. I'd been impressed by his single-minded focus on saving her. He'd given no thought to his own safety—or ours.

Confirms what I sensed earlier: he's in love with her. Just hope he doesn't get hurt. His grandmother was right. He's a good kid.

I watched as several cops boarded the Coast Guard cutter. I assumed they'd interview the crew.

I turned my attention back to Masa.

"Please join me in my cruiser for the trip to headquarters. We will need a statement from you on this morning's events." Always proper and polite, I wondered if he ever got flustered.

As soon as we were on Kam Highway headed toward Honolulu, Masa said, "We owe you a great deal for the information about Liquid Excitement. When we reached the factory, the owner, Jake Bradley, had to hunt for the key to the recycle bin and finally located it in the room behind the double plastic curtains."

"That must be Cho's clean area. I was told no one was allowed in there because of the potential of dust contamination."

"That may not have been the only reason." Masa skirted around a slow car, then continued. "We discovered a large freezer. The owner indicated that he'd never seen it before. It was nearly empty, but there were traces of a substance that looked like blood. We've sent samples to the lab for testing."

I wondered if it might be Philip's blood or maybe it belonged to a shark.

"Once he had the key, Mr. Bradley opened the bin. It appeared to be filled with foam dust and scraps. However, when we explored beneath the top layer, we discovered several burlap sacks containing shark fins. They were frozen, and the foam provided insulation to preserve them. We speculate they had been stored in the freezer at the factory."

In all the excitement, I'd forgotten about the ones on Tommy's boat. "Masa, there's another bag in the fresh water tank on the Boston Whaler. We put it there for safekeeping. One of the guys threw it overboard while we were chasing them, and Slade went in after it. It has fins in it, too."

Masa radioed to let the cops at the dock know where to look. "I appreciate your assistance." he said as he replaced the mike. "I believe we may have enough evidence for a conviction if today's witnesses corroborate our theory."

"Glad to help. I have a question, however. I know the car keeping an eye on Nicki and Philip's grandparents belongs to your department. Why are they there? And why did they follow me?"

Masa smiled. "After the murder, we had no idea if there might be a threat to the rest of the victim's family. We positioned surveillance teams to cover the grandparents and the parents. When you arrived, we wanted to make certain you would not be harmed."

"Thanks. I'm sure the senator will appreciate knowing that. He's very suspicious of your department. By the way, you were right. Not only was the rental car bugged, so was my room."

He nodded sagely.

"Have you learned anything else about Philip's murder," I asked.

"Nothing," he answered.

"I have a hunch it's connected to the poaching ring, but I don't know how. Maybe he stumbled upon their operation like Nicki probably did."

"Quite possible," he said. "But the two may not be related at all."

I'd hoped he'd uncovered something linking the crimes, and my spirits dropped to learn he hadn't.

Afraid I'm here a while longer. My daydream of relaxing with Gerry tonight in the hot tub melted away like shave ice on a hot day.

As we neared the city, we spotted Jamie's van ahead. The officer had apparently driven slower than Masa. Of course, he didn't have a siren or lights like we did. The van couldn't easily be identified as a law enforcement vehicle.

Masa dropped me off in front of the building, right behind the van. "I'll meet you inside. Have a seat. I will come for you when I'm ready for your statement." He drove off.

I waited on the sidewalk as Jamie's chair rolled off the ramp. An officer stood on each side. I followed them into the building.

As we entered, a couple rushed up to Jamie. The small dark-haired woman, who had obviously been crying, asked, "Why, Jamie? Why?"

Jamie raised his head and looked at them. "It was exciting."

"Exciting!" said the man.

"Yeah, Dad, exciting. Ever since the accident, it's been really boring. Nothing gave me the same kick as surfing used to. When Cho and Wacko roped me into this, I started to feel alive again."

The woman I assumed was his mother began to sob, and the father put an arm around her.

A man in an expensive-looking suit rushed up to the three of them. "Not another word, young man," he commanded. "I'm Scott Howland, representing Mr. Aiku-Howe." He presented his card to one of the officers. "Is there somewhere private where I can consult with my client?"

The officer led the group away.

I sat down heavily on a bench.

Excitement. Jake told me Jamie was foolhardy and careless. Said that's how he was injured in the first place. And once again, he'll pay for that excitement. What a waste.

As if thinking of him conjured up the man himself, Jake walked down the hall toward me.

"'Morning," he said as he settled heavily next to me. He looked like he'd been sucker punched. "It is still morning, isn't it? I can't believe it." He shook his head. "The recycling program seemed perfect. I had no idea what was going on. And it's my business. I should have spent more time watching the guys." He rocked forward and cupped his head as if he had a headache.

"How could you?" I asked. "From what I can figure out, the operation was pretty slick."

He looked up at me. "I knew Cho was too good to be true. He came along just when we lost our glasser. And he made such a production of keeping his area free from dust and debris. I know how messy Wacko is, and I was very impressed. I should have checked his background better."

"You think Cho was the leader?"

He thought about it for a second. "I think he worked for his uncle Lee. Cho brought him to us with the recycling idea. Said most of the shops on the island were already taking part. It made good economic and environmental sense. But I had no idea there was anything else to it."

I suddenly felt as tired as Jake looked. "I'll bet there's a cup of coffee around here somewhere. Probably vending machine swill, but I could use a little caffeine. How about you?"

"Sounds good to me."

We stood up and started down the hall.

"They told me to stick around. Said they'd probably have more questions after they talk to the guys. I feel as though I've been through a prize fight and came away without the trophy."

Some instinct led me to a couple of vending machines. Don't ask how I knew where to find them. We put in our money and made our selections.

Jake decided on a cola. He took a swig. "Ah, that tastes good. I needed something. Thanks."

I pulled my half-filled cup from the coffee machine. *Why don't you ever get a full cup, especially when you push the buttons for cream and sugar?* I sipped. It was hot and rather tasteless.

"I sure hope the cops believe me," Jake said as we walked back toward the entrance. "So far, they seem to. But you never know."

I just nodded in response. I didn't think Jake was involved, but until all the evidence was in, I decided to withhold judgment.

Our bench was still unoccupied, so we sat back down.

"Oh, God. I just realized. If all three of them are arrested and jailed, there's no one to work at the shop. How am I going to keep my business going?" Jake asked, looking stricken again. "What in hell did I do to deserve this?"

I knew no answer was expected, and I couldn't have come up with one anyway.

A couple of minutes later, a female officer approached. "Mr. Jones?"

"Yes."

"Mr. Watanabe would like to see you now. Please follow me."

I stood, nodded goodbye to Jake, and followed her down the hall.

Chapter 26: Confession

On the way to Masa's office, I tried to put the pieces together.

Did Philip stumble on the shark finning operation? Was that why he was killed? If so, were the North Shore developers involved? It seemed unlikely. Did Nicki see or hear something she shouldn't have? And if she did, how? Once they had her, what were the guys planning to do with her?

Then I remembered the day I'd walked into the shop through a door that was supposed to be locked.

Jake said Wacko was supposed to fix it. Did Philip or Nicki get in the same way? Or did something else altogether happen?

I was still pondering the possibilities when I entered Masa's office.

"Thank you," he said as he stood to offer his hand across his desk. "I would like one of my officers to take your statement here for privacy. Would that be all right with you?"

"Of course. This is your case. I only hope to corroborate the evidence your department found."

I'd been in his shoes before. The case belonged to the local jurisdiction. I was only there as special investigator to assist them. Besides, I wanted to stay out of the spotlight, and I didn't want Gerry to know how involved I'd been. I decided Masa should be the hero.

He picked up the phone. "We're ready now," he said.

I gave my statement. It was read back for approval and then taken to be transcribed for signature.

Masa sat back in his chair. "Mr. Wackenhut will be questioned shortly if you wish to observe."

"I would, thanks."

"Come with me." Masa led the way down the hall. "Mr. Aiku-Howe and the Lees have lawyers, so we may not get much information from them. But Mr. Wackenhut has remained in isolation. He appears to be in need of a drug fix, and I've been told the young man is ready to talk."

From what I'd heard when he came off the boat, I suspected Masa was right.

He led the way into the observation room. Through the one-way glass, we'd be able to see and hear everything without the suspect knowing we were there.

"We make audio and video recordings of all interrogations," Masa said.

I nodded. I had a chance to take in the room on the other side of the glass and noticed the comfortable-looking seats and soft, indirect lighting. What a difference from the old fashioned metal folding chairs and single glaring ceiling lamp I remembered from my early years on the force. I could also tell that the fixtures gave a more even illumination and probably created clearer images.

The door swung open, and Wacko was escorted to the table in handcuffs. One of the two officers closed the door, then joined the other opposite the suspect.

Before he even sat down, Wacko was already talking.

"It was an accident, man. Like, I didn't mean to do it. Everything was Cho's fault, ya know. His uncle dreamed it up. I just went along. But I didn't mean to kill anybody. You gotta believe me."

This was all rattled off quickly as if Wacko needed to get his story out as fast as possible.

"Mr. Wackenhut…" the heavier of the two officers began.

"It's Wacko, man. My dad, wherever the hell he is, is 'Mr. Wackenhut.'"

"Wacko, then. Please start at the beginning."

"Uh, let's see. I started working for Jake a few years ago. Don't remember exactly. Memory's not too good for dates."

"You said you didn't mean to kill anyone, that it was an accident. Who was the victim?"

The thin cop just sat and waited. I figured they might use the bad-cop/good-cop routine if things got dicey.

"Flip. But, man, I didn't mean to kill him. I was only trying, like, to scare him. And I didn't know it was him. Please! I'm telling ya the truth."

"Mr.…uh, Wacko, how did the accident happen?"

"We came in from a fishing run. Cho took the bag to his

area to put in the freezer. I waited for Jamie. Sometimes he needs help, ya know. Then we, like, went into the factory. We used the parking lot lights to see where we were going and didn't, like, turn the inside ones on until the door was closed. Didn't want to call attention, ya know."

I could see his hands shaking and thought he probably did need a fix.

"Then what happened?"

"I waited for Jamie to get his chair into the hall before I closed the door. So he could, like, see, ya know. I had my knife in my hand. Had to be careful no one stole the goods. Never thought I'd use it." He shook his head through the whole explanation, like he was trying to shake away the memory the way we used to shake an Etch-a-Sketch to clear the screen.

"What happened next?"

Still nothing from the slender officer.

"I closed the door. It was supposed to lock, man. Took a couple of steps, then it banged open. Scared the crap outta me. All I saw was a big guy in the doorway. I figured we were followed. Maybe a fishermen who brought us fins, or the black shirts, ya know. They been gettin' suspicious. Think they want a cut of the action."

"You didn't see the person's face?"

"No, man. It was dark inside. All I saw was a big black shape that started coming at me. I yelled, 'Stop,' but the guy didn't say anything. 'Don't make me use this,' I said, but he kept comin'. I pushed the knife, ya know, like I was going to stab him. Honest, man, I didn't mean to really do it, but he stepped right into it."

He shook even more and closed his eyes. "I think I'm gonna barf."

The quiet officer left the room and returned with a plastic pail and a soda. "Use this if you need it." He set the bucket next to Wacko's chair. "And this may settle your stomach," he said, opening the can.

Wacko took a big swig. "Thanks, man. They said I'd get some help if I answered all your questions. Feel really rotten." He closed his eyes. By now he was shaking all over. Then his eyes snapped open. "You gotta help me. No matter what Cho and Jamie say, it was an accident."

"What happened next?" the interrogator continued unemotionally.

"Cho closed the door. Then he turned on the light. That's when I knew it was Flip. But, man, the guy didn't say anything, ya know. How the hell was I supposed to know it was him?"

"What did you do next?"

"Cho checked him over. Said he was dead. I asked what we were gonna do. Man, I was freakin'. Cho said we could put Flip's body in the bin. The ship would pick it up in a couple a days. But we couldn't just carry him out to dump him. He was too floppy, ya know. Cho said to get his board, so I got it from his car."

"What did you do with that?" the officer asked.

"We loaded him on and wrapped the leash around his

legs. Then Jamie started cryin' and said we had to put the leash on his ankle, like the board would get away without it. It didn't make no sense, but we did it to shut him up. The kid was losin' it."

Wacko stopped to take a swig of his soda. "I still think I'm gonna barf."

"That's what the pail's for," said the other guy.

"Please continue," the questioner pressed on. I recognized the technique. Don't give him time to think about his answers.

"Jamie was no use, so Cho and I dragged Flip out to the bin and dumped him in. Then we got all the foam in the place and put it on top of him."

He took another gulp and picked up the bucket. Then he put it down.

"The body was in the bin, and then..."

Wacko put his head down and groaned. Then he took a couple of deep breaths and said, "Cho said to take Flip's car somewhere and wipe it down, then dump it. So I drove and Jamie followed. When we finished, we came back to the shop."

"What did you find when you returned?"

"Cho cleaned up all the blood. Geez, the place stunk with bleach, but the big spots were gone. Then we, like, closed up and went home."

"How did the victim's body get to Maui?"

"Don't know, man. They picked up the bin on Friday, like always. Then we heard the news the next morning. I don't know. I swear."

"Is there anything else you'd like to tell us about his death?"

"Nothin' more to tell. That's, like, what happened. He walked into the knife. I just wanted to scare him, and he walked right into it."

The cops glanced at the notes they'd brought in with them. Then the quiet one said, "Tell us what happened with Ms. Weaver."

"We were out collectin' fins last night. Came back and, like, unlocked the door. We took our haul inside and closed up. I needed a fix and didn't want to wait until Cho's uncle brought our money. But Cho said we had to do it the old man's way. We kinda started to fight. Don't remember everything, but I think Cho said something about remembering the last time we got careless. Maybe he said something about Flip, too."

Wacko picked up the plastic container and bent his head over it and gagged, but nothing happened. In a few seconds, he put it back on the floor and drank more cola.

"We heard a noise. Flip's girlfriend was hiding behind the shipping boxes. Don't know how much she heard, but we couldn't let her go, ya know. So we like tied her up until we could figure it out. We didn't hurt her, I swear, man. Cho called his uncle who said the boat would be off the coast in the morning, and we should just take her out there. That's what we were doin'. Don't know what the old man was thinkin' but we had to get her out of the factory, ya know, before Jake got there."

"Was he involved in any of this?"

"Hell, no, man. Jake's like a straight arrow. But he's not around much. Cho sweet-talked him, ya know, to throw him off. He didn't have a clue."

Wacko took a big drink, burped loudly, and wiped his mouth on the back of his hand. "Whoa, that felt better." He burped again.

"So you took Ms. Weaver where?"

"To Jamie's boat. We saw Slade on the dock, but he couldn't catch us. We just got out of the harbor when this other boat started comin' up on us. Couldn't tell who the hell it was. Thought it might be the black shirts tryin' to get in on our deal, so we tried to outrun 'em. But they were catchin' up. Cho pulled a gun. Jamie and me didn't know he had it. He fired but missed. Guess it scared 'em 'cause they slowed down. Scared me, too."

He stopped, took a deep breath, and closed his eyes. "Gettin' a little dizzy."

Neither of the cops reacted. They just sat and waited.

Finally, he started talking again. "Figured we better dump the bag of fins overboard in case the cops got wind of anything. There's a pick-up spot where the other fishermen dump their fins. It's on the shelf before the drop off. Knew we could come back and get 'em later when no one was around. But then we saw somebody go in after the bag. Man, that guy was nuts.

"We kept goin'. Cho said if we could get to international

waters, they couldn't touch us. Said we had to get Nicki to the ship. Once the fins and the girl were gone, we'd be in the clear. But the crazy guys in the other boat started comin' up fast again. Cho took a couple more shots. When I told him I thought he was nuts, he turned the gun toward me. Man, he had an insane look. Scared the crap outta me."

"What was Jamie doing at this time?" asked the quiet one.

"Just, like, drivin' the boat, man. He won't let nobody else run the thing. But I could tell Cho scared him."

Wacko went on to tell about the Coast Guard catching them. Since we were there when it happened, I already knew the rest. But we still didn't know how Philip got to Maui or exactly how Nicki got involved.

"They will continue to question him for a while," Masa said. "Your statement should be ready by now." He led me out of the observation room.

"At least we know Nicki's okay and how Philip died," I observed.

Masa nodded.

I signed the statement, and Masa asked if I wanted to phone the senator.

"No," I answered. "This is your case, and you broke it."

"Thank you." He nodded. "For everything." Then he asked me to wait outside a while longer in case they needed me.

I felt completely drained and suddenly realized just how tired I was. I stopped by the vending machine and got a Coke. Watching Wacko reminded me I was still thirsty. The half cup of java hadn't perked me up like I'd hoped.

When I returned to the familiar bench, I found Slade there. Jake was gone.

"How're you doing, son?" I asked as I sat down. My leg had started to throb, and I needed to sit awhile.

The young man looked as though he'd been up many hours. Come to think of it, he had been. Dark circles framed his red-rimmed eyes; his face was shadowed with stubble, and his hair stuck up. I watched as he ran his hands through it.

"They're questioning Nicki," he explained.

"How is she?"

"The EMTs checked her out. Other than a few bruises, she'll be okay. But she was really scared. So was I."

I placed a hand on his shoulder. "I was, too."

"On the way over here, she told me she knew she wouldn't sleep last night, so she went to the factory. She found the door unlocked and went inside. She had a flashlight and looked around. Then she heard a key in the lock. So she hid behind a big pile of boxes." He shook his head. "I wish she'd just waited for me. I said I'd go with her this morning. But, no. She had to do it alone."

"Don't blame yourself. I know you'd have done anything to keep her out of danger. You care too much about her."

"How did you know?"

"I've seen how you look at her. You went into the water to save her. And you told me if you'd met her first, you'd have been interested."

"Oh yeah." He took a breath. "Nicki heard them talking.

Said it sounded like Wacko killed Flip. He and Cho were arguing. Anyway, she must have made a noise because they found her. The guys tied her up. Then they started talking about what to do with her. She said Cho called somebody. Then they dumped her onto Jamie's spare wheelchair and took her out to his boat. She heard me call to her, but I couldn't get there in time."

Slade dropped his head into his hands.

"You did everything you could. Calling me was quick thinking. Good thing Tommy and I were close."

He looked up. "Yeah. Thanks. I don't know what would have happened if…" He couldn't bring himself to finish the sentence.

"But we were there. And Tommy has a fast boat."

He nodded. "I decided something today."

"What's that?"

"I want to go to the academy and become a police officer. When I was a kid, I talked about it a lot, but Dad never believed me. Today I felt more alive than I have in a long time. I want to do something to help other people."

"If you need a recommendation, ask. I think you'd do well in law enforcement."

"Thanks. I hope you're right."

My phone rang. It was the senator. "We'll be outside headquarters in a few minutes. Please meet us there. And thank you." He hung up.

I wondered what would happen next.

Chapter 27: Headed Home

I left Slade sitting on the bench and walked to the main entrance. In a minute or two, the familiar limousine with the etched windows pulled up. The front passenger door opened and Terry emerged carrying a canvas bag. He then opened the rear door, reached in, and helped Mrs. Fowler out. She was followed by the senator. The steps were crowded with reporters and photographers snapping away. Terry kept saying, "The senator and the police will conduct a joint press conference shortly," as he parted the press. Senator and Mrs. Fowler followed him to the landing.

"Come inside," Terry said to me. He took my arm so I could enter with him. Officers surrounded our party and escorted us through the doors.

Once we were inside, the senator shook my hand. "Thank you for everything you've done. Clarence has a check for you in the car. He'll meet you around back."

He stepped away, and Keilani reached out to hug me. Then she kissed my cheek. "We'll never be able to repay you," she whispered.

"The police solved the case," I said.

She smiled. "That's what we plan to say. But we're aware of the enormous role you played." Then she moved closer and whispered, "Thank you for keeping your promise. You cleared my son and restored him to our family."

"He's a fine young man, just as you said."

As she nodded, I noticed a sheen in her eyes and the hint of unshed tears.

"But I didn't..." I started.

She put a finger against her lips, whispered, "Shh," turned, and followed her husband down the hall.

Terry remained with me.

"What's in the bag?" I asked.

"Clean clothes and toiletries for Slade. Do you know where he is?"

"It so happens I do." I led him to the bench where the young man still sat, head in hands.

"Your dad wants you to clean up and change," Terry told him gently.

His head popped up. "What about Nicki?"

"Your grandparents are bringing her things. They should be here soon."

Slade hesitated, then accepted the package and walked off.

Terry turned back to me. "Kid's got it bad."

I nodded. "I saw your exit with the contingent from California last night," I said. Then I laughed, and Terry joined me.

"Put them on a plane early this morning," he said. "Can't say I'll miss them."

"I can imagine."

"Guess you heard about Bob Hillman."

"No. What happened?"

"When the senator heard he'd gotten Slade involved with the developers, he confronted the guy. Bob said he didn't see anything wrong with it. Said it was Slade's choice and his decision. Then Senator Fowler asked him about the conversation Phil overheard on the phone the night he disappeared. Bob denied he was threatening Slade but admitted that the corporate honchos were putting pressure on him to deliver the votes. The senator fired him on the spot, and I got the job."

"Sounds like a good move. Congratulations, I hope."

"Thanks, I hope." Terry grinned. "I need to return the yacht keys to Doc and Naomi this afternoon after the chaos dies down. Mrs. Fowler never liked using it, and the senator decided he'll campaign on land from now on."

The same female officer who had taken me to Masa's office approached. "Mr. Jones, I was asked to let you know you're free to go."

"Thanks."

"If you need a ride, Clarence can take you," Terry offered. "The press conference won't start for at least another hour, and we'll probably be here awhile after that."

"Are you sure?"

"Yeah. You earned it."

"Thanks. I need to see Clarence anyway. Want me to return the keys for you? I'll be headed back to the North Shore."

"That would help a lot. Thanks." He handed them to me.

Slade came toward us in clean clothes. He'd obviously shaved but still looked haggard.

"Let's go find your folks," Terry suggested.

"And Nicki," Slade added.

"And Nicki," Terry repeated.

"Goodbye, Mr. Jones," Slade said as he shook my hand.

"After everything we've been through, I think you could call me Agapé, don't you?"

"Hope to see you again, Agapé." He waved and followed Terry.

I found Clarence in the back lot, smoking and leaning against the limo.

"Hi, Clarence," I said.

"Glad you're okay," he replied, looking me up and down.

"Just fine except for a sore leg and exhaustion." I laughed.

He nodded seriously, dropped his cigarette, and ground it out. "Want to ride shotgun?" he asked, pointing to the front passenger door.

I grinned. "Much better than being in the back alone."

He opened the door for me, then went around and got in on the driver's side.

"Oh, I have something for you." He reached into his inside coat pocket and withdrew a legal-size brown envelope.

As he started the engine, I looked inside.

"Whoa. This is more than we agreed on." It was a lot more.

Clarence put the car in gear and started out. "Senator and Mrs. Fowler are very grateful to you for uncovering Philip's murderer."

"But the police..."

"The family is aware of law enforcement's involvement, and they also know you discovered critical evidence." He skillfully maneuvered into traffic.

"Yes, but..."

"But the senator finally has answers, and Mrs. Fowler is grateful for the peace of mind."

"I'm glad they feel that way, but I really don't deserve..."

We stopped for a light, and Clarence turned to me. "You may not want to admit your part in it, but Slade and his dad are speaking. Mrs. Fowler gives you the credit. Did you know the senator offered Slade a job?"

"No."

"'Course, he turned it down. Bet you could've predicted that."

I nodded.

We pulled onto the freeway and enjoyed the drive. I filled Clarence in on everything I felt free to divulge. He'd learn the rest soon enough.

I told him my car was at the harbor, so we parked there.

"You don't have to get out, Clarence. I'll be fine," I said

as I reached for the door.

He put a restraining hand on my shoulder. “Yes, I do, Mr. Jones. It’s my job.”

He got out and held the door open for me. Then he took my hand in his big paw. “Take care.”

“You, too.” I watched as he drove away.

I walked to the Cobalt and called Doc. Naomi picked up on the first ring.

“Terry asked me to deliver the yacht keys. Would this be a good time?”

“Come right up. I’ll buzz you in at the main gate.”

I drove up to the house, once again amazed at how it fit into its surroundings.

Naomi came out to meet me.

“So good to see you.” She gave me a hug. “Doc’s inside waiting for you.”

“Here’s the keys.” I handed them to her as we entered.

“Maybe it’s time we thought about selling the boat. We never use it.” She laughed. “We’d rather be in a dinky outrigger wearing ourselves out paddling.”

I laughed with her.

She may be rich, but she’s so down to earth. She reminds me of Gerry.

I was suddenly anxious to get back home to my sweetheart.

“Would you like a glass of lemonade?” Naomi asked as Doc entered the room.

“No, thanks—”

"Agapé," Doc interrupted and greeted me. "Will you be joining us for practice tomorrow morning?"

"Afraid not. I'm headed out today, as soon as I can book a flight."

"Keilani called to tell us about the press conference. You were napping, honey."

"What press conference?" Doc looked at me.

"We had quite a day," I told him.

"Don't put the detective on the spot," Naomi cautioned. "But you could turn on the TV so we can all watch it together."

"Much as I'd like to join you, I need to get back, pack, and check out," I told her.

She nodded, and Doc left the room. "Before you go, we have a little something for you to take back to Maui. Well, actually, Doc has something for you."

He returned holding a brown package, withdrew something, and handed it to me. It was one of his paintings.

"It's the same view as you had from your room at Turtle Bay," he said. And it was.

"I don't know what to say," I started. "It's gorgeous."

Naomi put her hand on my arm. "We wanted to give you a memento of your time here on the North Shore, so you'll always remember."

"I'll treasure this, and I can't wait to show it to my wife. She'll love it. I didn't get her anything and had planned to stop in one of the airport stores for a little something. This is so much better."

"We also want you to come back and spend a few days here with us. You appreciated the architecture and said you wanted your wife to see it." Naomi looked at me earnestly.

"We'd love to come. Thanks for the invitation."

"Don't think you can get out of it, now," she said as she walked me to the door. I heard the sound of the TV behind me. "I'll haunt you if I need to."

"Don't worry. This is one offer too good to refuse or ignore."

She kissed me on the cheek. "Take care. And I appreciate my dear friend's happiness at finally seeing her son and his father forming an adult relationship. Even though she's lost one son, and she may never get over it, the tension in the house has lightened. And she believes you were the catalyst."

I didn't know what to say, so I nodded and walked back to my car.

All the way to the hotel, I questioned my real contribution to the case. Most of the time I was confused and without a clue.

'Honey, you finally put all the pieces together, just like you always do.' Lovey's voice sounded in my head.

Well, I didn't really solve the case.

'Oh, but son, you gave the police the lead they needed. And that's what you were here for.'

Maybe you're right.

'I know I'm right! And you said you'd help that nice young man, too.'

I will. He really is a good kid, just like his mother and grandmother said.

'Don't you forget, mothers always know best. Son, I'm so proud of you. Always have been. Always will be. Oh, and I love you. But then, you knew that.'

I heard her chuckle fade away.

I made my way to my room, filled my suitcase, carefully padding the painting in the middle of my clothing to protect it. Then I took one last look around. The view was still spectacular, but seeing my Gerry held even more appeal. I phoned the airline and reserved a seat on the next flight. The timing should be perfect. Then I called home to let my bride know my arrival time.

* * * *

When I got home, the news conference was being shown on every channel. All I wanted to do was soak in the hot tub with Gerry, but she was anxious to know all about the case.

She'd fixed us an early dinner. Good thing, since I'd missed lunch. I had a snack at the airport, but the selection was meager. I figured she wouldn't have been thrilled by the chips. But she didn't ask, so I didn't tell her.

Detective Watanabe handled the press conference in his usual calm, matter-of-fact way. He also answered one of my last questions.

"This afternoon, law enforcement boarded a Chinese ship anchored off the coast of Oahu. The crew was questioned about the body of Philip Fowler. Two of them confessed that they discovered the body in a container on board the ship late Friday night. They have stated that they threw the body and the surfboard, to which it was attached, into the ocean off the coast of Maui out of fear that they would be charged with the murder. Fortunately, the body was discovered before the sharks that frequent the area found it."

He went on to explain that the two crewmen would be charged as accessories after the fact.

It was the only question I still had, and I was relieved to have it answered. I was sure the Fowlers were, too.

Later in the hot tub, with the jets loosening the muscles of my sore leg, Gerry kissed me. "I'm so glad you weren't in the middle of this one. It sounds so dangerous! But I still don't understand why the senator paid you so much."

"Honey, he's from a very wealthy family. I'm sure he and his wife were relieved that Philip's body was recovered. It might not have been had the sharks gotten to it."

She shuddered even though the water was steaming. "I just can't imagine how that poor woman is able to handle losing her son. I keep thinking about Martin..."

I put an arm around her. "He's safe at home. I do hope you'll get a chance to meet Keilani. You'd like her, and her parents."

"Maybe when we visit the doctor and his wife in a couple of months."

Good as her word, Naomi had already phoned to make arrangements.

"And I can't believe they gave us that gorgeous painting." She'd already hung it over the TV. "Did your room really have that view?"

"It sure did," I told her. I put an arm around her and

pulled her close. Then I kissed her. "I really missed you."

"I missed you, too, honey."

"I'll show you everything when we go back. And I'd really like you to meet the folks I got to know."

We sat comfortably enjoying being together. And that's exactly where I wanted to be, back home with Gerry where I belonged.

Epilogue

Three Months Later

It was still dark when I pulled up at the canoe club. I hadn't slept much the night before and found myself wide awake at four o'clock. I got up quietly so I wouldn't disturb Gerry, pulled on my trunks, and kissed her goodbye.

Today was our last outrigger practice before the big race. We did really well in the last competition, and we all believed we stood a chance of winning this one.

I took the steaming cup of Starbucks coffee, purchased on the way, and strolled across the sand to the weathered picnic table near the club's banyan tree. I sat on the bench and gazed at the still-dark sea. The sky behind me would lighten soon, and I looked forward to watching the rays illuminate the ocean.

Maybe it was because of the email I received from Nicki the night before, or perhaps because we'd been to visit Doc and Naomi a couple of weeks earlier, but I remembered another early morning before a paddle. A morning that went terribly wrong and enmeshed me in a case I'd rather forget. Finding the body of a handsome young surfer who had everything going for him, whose life was cut short far too soon, still haunted me.

Working as a special investigator on the case took me to Oahu and into a confusing and dangerous situation. Unlike that experience, my return, this time with my bride, was a real vacation.

When Gerry met Mano and Malia, they quickly told her how grateful they were for my contribution to finding Philip's killer. I had a heck of a time convincing my wife that it was the police who'd cracked the case. Still, I think she suspected I was more involved than I'd let on.

When Malia heard I was returning to Oahu, she and Mano insisted we come for dinner. Mano made his famous *huli-huli* chicken, and their entire family showed up. It was like a much smaller version of the luau after the paddle-out, except Gerry and I were the guests of honor. Doc and Naomi had been invited as well, but were unable to join us.

As I watched the family dynamic, it was clear the senator was proud of Slade. The Fowlers seemed much happier than when I first met them, although Keilani still had the haunted look. I suspect she'll probably wear it the rest of her life. She and Gerry hit it off right away, just as I expected.

Malia and Mano 'talked story' about growing up on the North Shore, and Gerry was fascinated. They showed her Mano's surfing photos and the one of the old Hale'iwa Hotel with Malia as a young girl.

As promised, I'd sent them copies of the shots I took the evening of the paddle-out, and Gerry was shown those as well.

While the couple entertained my wife, I had a chance to talk to Slade.

"I've been accepted at the Academy and can't wait to start," Slade told me, "Thanks for the letters you wrote. Detective Watanabe said you sent one to him, too."

"You earned it," I told him.

"Heck, I didn't do anything you wouldn't have done."

I laughed. "Maybe when I was a youngster like you. But I've become more cautious in my old age."

"You're not old," he protested.

"Young man, have you had your eyes checked lately? They won't let you in if they're too bad. And yours obviously are."

We had a good laugh, and it pleased me to see him happy.

"What are you doing now?" I asked.

"Until classes start, I've been working in the shop with Jake. After all, I am a partner. But now I'm a working partner. Oh, and I've got the 'Big Machine' wired and can turn out more boards than Wacko ever did. It's really kind of a kick seeing those perfect blanks come out. But it's not what I want to do for the rest of my life."

Mano came over to update me on his activities. He hadn't lost his passion for fighting major development as a member of the 'Keep the North Shore Country' group.

"Those sneaky developers are still trying to build way too much on the north end of the island. It can't support the growth. We finally got the courts to rule that a new environmental impact study is needed. That should hold them off for a while."

It was clear Mano had lost none of his spunk. In fact, he seemed to stand straighter and walk easier.

He updated me on the other local activities. The black shirts were still intimidating the surfers, and Nicki still worked at the hospital. In short, nothing much had changed.

I could see that Nicki and Slade seemed even closer than they were before I left. I thought Malia might get her wish for Nicki as a granddaughter yet.

We left that evening, full and happy.

"It was like visiting with old friends. Or even family," Gerry remarked in the car on our way back to the Schwencks' house.

"That's how I felt when I met them. They're good people."

We drove the short distance with the windows down, listening to the lullaby of the ocean and watching the stars. I had to admit, Mano had a point. By this time of night, the road was nearly deserted. More construction would bring heavier traffic, and the atmosphere would surely be different.

Naomi had given me the security code, so when we reached the gate, I punched it in.

"How on earth did you find this road?" Gerry asked. "I'd have missed it."

"It's hard enough in the daytime, let alone at night. But I've been here several times and remember the way."

The lights were on as we drove up in front of the house.

Gerry sighed and said, "It's really beautiful."

I knew no response was required.

Staying at Naomi and Doc's house was better than my first brief tour. The sea breeze flowed through the open areas, and the views were even more spectacular than I remembered. All four bedrooms were *en suite*, and each was decorated in Hawaiian prints with Doc's original paintings on the walls.

The next morning at breakfast, Gerry greeted Naomi with, "This is way better than any hotel."

Her appreciation made our hostess smile. "That's the reason Johnny and I built it. We wanted to share this little piece of Paradise with others, as well as enjoy it ourselves. Doc and I've already arranged to leave the property to the state when we're both gone."

I guess we looked confused because she added, "Since neither of us ever had children, we'd like to see the house become an art gallery or museum. And if they decide to hang some of Doc's paintings…well…" Then she laughed, making a lovely tinkling sound.

"Coffee?" she asked.

We went to church with Doc and Naomi at Kawaiaha'o where the funeral had been held. The building was beautiful, matched only by the glorious sound of the choir. Somehow, even familiar hymns sung in Hawaiian are even more beautiful.

We ate lunch at Duke's Canoe Club in Waikiki and watched the surfers and the outriggers enjoying the midday waves.

Later that day, we drove to Turtle Bay, and I showed Gerry my room. She was impressed.

"I just wish you'd been with me, sweetheart," I said. Then I kissed her as we enjoyed the same view depicted in the painting now hanging in our living room, only this time it was for real.

"After seeing this place, so do I! But while you were gone, Chuck and Maggie kept me busy. And I had my class. I'm just glad you didn't stay any longer."

We walked hand-in-hand along the shore away from other guests. I remembered calling from that spot and wondered if the bugs were still in my room. We sat in the sand to watch the sun set.

When we got back, Doc asked if I wanted to paddle with his team the next morning, so I went. My wife slept in. Naomi decided to stay home to keep Gerry company and arrange for breakfast.

It was good to see everyone again. I finally met Georgia. She was the member whose place I'd taken.

We paddled nearly to Dillingham and back. While putting the equipment away, I had a chance to talk to Terry.

"How's the new job going?"

"Crazy busy, what with the election coming up." He grinned. "But I like it a lot. Especially without Bob around."

"Or the ex-girlfriend and the senator's parents?"

We both laughed at that.

"You bet!"

Terry had to get to his office in Honolulu, and the rest had plans as well, so Doc and I were the only ones headed back for breakfast. It was a repeat of the first time, with custom-made omelets, fresh fruit, pastries—the works. Only this time, I ate a bit more carefully. Gerry was watching, and she seemed to approve of my choices.

As we left, Naomi made us promise we'd come back again, and Gerry assured them we'd love to have them as our guests on Maui.

"We might very well take you up on that," said Naomi as she kissed and hugged us both.

"After being here, the beautiful painting in our living room has much more meaning," Gerry told Doc. "We can't thank you enough for everything."

"I paint because I enjoy it. And if other people appreciate what I create, well, that adds even more pleasure."

We watched them wave goodbye until our car turned the bend and they disappeared from sight.

"I like your friends," Gerry said. "All of them."

I smiled. I'd known she would.

After we flew home to Kihei, Masa phoned to tell me Wacko turned informant as part of a plea bargain for a reduced sentence.

"Bob Hillman was arrested for influence peddling and you were right. He had the devices placed in your car and in your room," he said. "His trial and those of Wacko, Jamie, and the others have been postponed."

"Thanks for letting me know," I said, glad about the outcome.

"It was a pleasure to work with you, Mr. Jones."

I figured it would probably be at least a year or two before the cases went to court. But I was confident the police had enough evidence for convictions.

The following week, Jake brought Mal's board with him to Maui. He'd arranged for a special airbrushed Hawaiian sunset paint job. It's pretty impressive, and I know Mal will love it. I wanted to send it to him right away, but Gerry said I had to wait until they came for Christmas.

"I found another glasser and am training a new sander," Jake told me. "Fortunately the big order for Japan was nearly finished before the arrests, so I'm confident the new guys will be up to speed before the next large order. Toshi says we're okay unless one of them can't cut it."

"Glad to hear it. Slade told me he's working for you, too."

"Yeah, he's getting real good with the volume shaper. I can't believe the change in him. He's really excited about coming to work and keeps talking about being a police officer. I've known him for a pretty long time, and I've never seen him like this before."

"I noticed he's much closer to his dad now."

"Seems that way."

We invited Jake to stay for dinner. I grilled salmon steaks, and Gerry made her famous Hawaiian fruit salad with papaya seed dressing. We ate on the lanai, and I remembered how much I'd missed being home.

* * * *

As I sat on the beach reminiscing, the sun began to highlight the waves before me, turning them from indigo to turquoise to aqua tipped in silver.

Once again, I reminded myself how lucky I was to be living in Paradise.

Then I heard cars arrive and got up to greet my team. One more practice before the big race, and this time we'd win!

ABOUT THE AUTHORS

Lorna Lund and Larry Collins were raised in Alhambra, California, where they attended grammar school and high school together. They've been married for forty-five years and have one daughter, Kimberly.

Larry is an engineer and spent many years working on various projects throughout the United States and around the world. Lorna was in Document Control and IT Change Management. She now works as a Technical Writer. They were both employed in Japan building the Universal Studios theme park. Larry was a Project Engineer, responsible for the Jurassic Park, JAWS, and WaterWorld attractions. Lorna put her documentation skills to use working in the Osaka field office.

They have written one memoir together, *31 Months in Japan: The Building of a Theme Park*, and *Murder... They Wrote*, a cozy mystery. Lorna also writes anthologies with three friends.